"Som...
between us, Susana."

"I'm not sure I believe, as my grandfather did, in love at first sight. I only know the thought of never seeing you again terrifies me."

"Armando..." Susan's throat worked with the need to cry. "We don't know anything about each other," she managed to say.

The moment was here; she had to tell him.

"I know all that I need to know."

"Please..." She stepped away from him. Hands pressed close to her sides, steeling herself, she said, "There's something I have to tell you. Something I should have told you before this."

"What is it, Susana?" Armando smiled. "Are you hiding a husband back in Texas? Do you have a secret lover? What is it, my dear?"

Susan looked up at him and knew she would have given her soul not to say the words that had to be said....

Dear Reader,

Welcome to the Silhouette **Special Edition** experience! With your search for consistently satisfying reading in mind, every month the authors and editors of Silhouette **Special Edition** aim to offer you a stimulating blend of deep emotions and high romance.

The name Silhouette **Special Edition** and the distinctive arch on the cover represent a commitment—a commitment to bring you six sensitive, substantial novels each month. In the pages of a Silhouette **Special Edition**, compelling true-to-life characters face riveting emotional issues—and come out winners. All the authors in the series strive for depth, vividness and warmth in writing these stories of living and loving in today's world.

The result, we hope, is romance you can believe in. Deeply emotional, richly romantic, infinitely rewarding—that's the Silhouette **Special Edition** experience. Come share it with us—six times a month! With this month's distinguished roster of gifted contemporary writers—Bay Matthews, Karen Keast, Barbara Faith, Madelyn Dohrn, Dawn Flindt and Andrea Edwards—you won't want to miss a single volume.

Best wishes,

Leslie Kazanjian,
Senior Editor

BARBARA FAITH
Choices of
the Heart

Silhouette Special Edition

Published by Silhouette Books New York

America's Publisher of Contemporary Romance

SILHOUETTE BOOKS
300 East 42nd St., New York, N.Y. 10017

ISBN: 0-373-09615-1

First Silhouette Books printing August 1990

Printed in the U.S.A.

BARBARA FAITH

is very happily married to an ex-matador she met when she lived in Mexico. After a honeymoon spent climbing pyramids in the Yucatán, they settled down in California—but they're vagabonds at heart. They travel at every opportunity, but Barbara always finds the time to write.

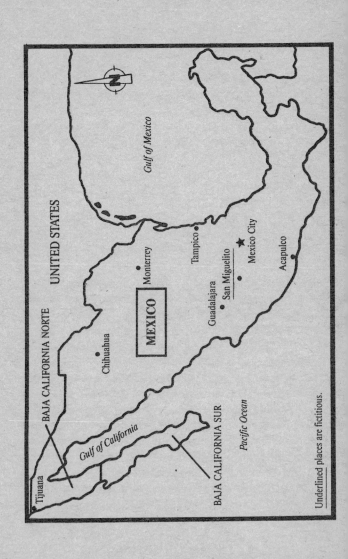

Underlined places are fictitious.

Chapter One

The air conditioning fizzled and died early in the morning of the second day, and the temperature in the train soared into the high eighties. Susan hadn't had any morning queasiness for more than a week, but with the heat and the rocking motion of the train, her stomach started doing warning flip-flops.

She looked out of the window and took a couple of deep breaths as the train sped around another curve and began climbing up into the mountains. The land had been dull and gray for the first few hours after they'd left Nuevo Laredo yesterday afternoon, but here in the mist-covered mountains of Mexico everything was greener. Pine trees and tropical flowers had replaced dry mesquite and cactus, and in the early-morning light small children waved from railway-siding shacks and old men led skinny, raw-boned mules through dried fields of corn.

What am I doing here? Susan wondered as she gazed out at the passing scenery. Maybe she should have stayed in Houston and found another job. Or gone back to Granbury. Instead, she'd decided on the small town in Mexico where Maria Mendoza lived.

She and Maria had been best friends as well as college roommates, and they'd shared an apartment in Houston for a year before Maria moved to Mexico. "I'm half Mexican and I've never been to Mexico," Maria had said. "It's time I got to know my father's country."

For the past year she'd been begging Susan to come for a visit. But Susan had always been too busy, first with her job, then with her father's lingering illness, and finally with Zachary.

Zachary. She leaned her face against the window and closed her eyes, trying to blot out all of her bitter thoughts of the man who was the reason for her leaving Houston.

She was so preoccupied that at first she didn't hear the porter knock on her door to announce that breakfast was being served in the dining room. But when he knocked again, she picked up her purse and opened the door of her roomette. Just as she did, the train swerved and she fell back against the door.

"*Cuidado.*" A chubby bear of a man with laugh lines around his mouth and a clerical collar around his throat grasped her arm to steady her. "Careful, *señorita*," he cautioned in a heavily accented voice. "We're in the mountains now."

"I haven't gotten my sea legs yet," Susan said when she regained her balance. "How far ahead is the dining car?"

"Only two cars. May I escort you there?"

Susan hesitated, then said, "Yes, thank you, Father."

"Just let me tell my friend that I'm going on ahead." He raised his hand to knock on the door of the roomette next to hers when the door opened.

"*¿Listas para comer?*" asked the tall man in his early thirties. Then he saw Susan and with a smile he said in English, "How do you manage it, *Padre*? I leave you alone and even with all the doors closed you manage to find the prettiest woman on the train. It's the clerical collar, isn't it? Instant trust. Remarkable."

The priest shook his head. "This ill-mannered fellow is Armando Cobian, *señorita*. I'm Father Ramiro de Santiago."

"Susan Alexander." She offered her hand, not sure now what to do. It might have been pleasant—and safe—having breakfast with the priest, but the other man was something else. He was macho male from the top of his black curly hair all the way down to his polished boots.

With a slight smile he looked her up and down, and his eyebrows, heavy black over Spanish-green eyes, notched up a quarter of an inch. In a voice as soft as hand-rubbed leather he said, "I'm delighted to meet you, *señorita*."

Susan stepped away from him and, turning to the priest, said, "Why don't you lead the way?"

But as they made their way through the two cars, it was the other man who had his hand on her arm, guiding her, steadying her whenever the train swayed. And when they reached the dining car, he pulled out a chair by the window for her and took the seat next to her.

"Where are you going, Señorita Alexander?" Father Ramiro asked while the waiter poured coffee for the two men and tea for Susan. "To Mexico City? Or perhaps on to Guadalajara?"

"No, I'm on my way to San Miguelito."

"Ah, that's where I'm going, too. San Miguelito is my home. Have you ever been there before?"

Susan shook her head. "I have a friend who lives there, Maria Mendoza. I'll be living in her house while she's in Spain."

"I've met Miss Mendoza," the priest said. "As a matter of fact, I have one of her paintings. It's unfortunate that she won't be in San Miguelito while you are. How long do you plan to stay?"

"Seven or eight months."

"Alone?" Armando frowned. "You're going to be living in San Miguelito alone? What do your parents think about that?"

"My parents are dead." Susan put her cup carefully down on the saucer. "My mother died when I was twelve. My father died six months ago. We... we were very close."

"That must have been difficult for you." Father Ramiro nodded sympathetically. "Do you have any brothers and sisters?"

"No. I have a cousin who lives in Hawaii, but we haven't kept in touch." She turned away to gaze out of the open window, putting an end to the questions.

The conversation went on around her. It seemed that Father Ramiro and Armando Cobian had known each other since they'd been boys in the same private school, and it was obvious they were good friends who enjoyed bantering with each other.

"Armando was a hellion," the priest told Susan. "The poor nuns could barely keep up with him."

"The poor nuns!" Armando snorted. "They did nothing but box my ears and keep me in after school."

"You deserved to be kept in."

"I did not! I was a model student."

"A model student?" Father Ramiro grinned at Susan. "He was in one scrape after another, Señorita Alexander. If he wasn't in a fight, then he was up to some other mischief. One Sunday before mass he drank some of the communion wine. Unfortunately it was the day the Monsignor had chosen to honor us by visiting. It was Armando's turn to ring the church bell. Just as the Monsignor entered the courtyard Armando grabbed the bell rope and with a bloodcurdling yell he swung out over the yard, his hair standing on end, a fiendish grin on his face."

The priest shook his head. "Model student indeed!" he said, joining in Susan's laughter.

She had a nice laugh, Armando thought. She looked very young, certainly too young to be traveling alone in a foreign country. He wondered where she was from and why she had decided to come to Mexico.

"Are you an artist?" he asked.

"No."

"A writer? There are several American writers living in San Miguelito."

Susan shook her head and her rich chestnut hair, blown by the breeze from the open window, drifted about her shoulders. "I'm a secretary," she said, and opened the menu.

Armando couldn't help watching her. When the waiter came, she ordered scrambled eggs, but when they were served she only pretended to eat. Her fingers were long and delicately slim, the nails polished a light shade of rose. She ate half a piece of toast and when she raised her teacup Armando saw that her hands were trembling.

She put the teacup down and leaned her head against her hand. "It's so hot," she said.

"It will be cooler in San Miguelito." The priest looked concerned. "Aren't you feeling well?"

Susan tried to smile. Then the smile faded and she clamped down hard on her lower lip. "I'll...I'll be all right if I can rest for a little while." She put some money on the table, then pushed her chair back. "It was nice meeting you, Father." She nodded at Armando. "Mr. Cobian."

Armando picked up the money and tried to hand it back to her. *"Por favor,"* he said. "Allow me to buy your breakfast."

"No," she said firmly. "Thank you, but no."

"Then let me help you back to your roomette." He stood up.

"I don't need any help." Susan's voice was sharper than she had intended it to be, and relenting she said, "But thank you."

If there was one thing she didn't need right now it was a Mexican Don Juan, Susan thought as she made her way back to her roomette. She'd had her fill of good-looking men. Of men. Period. The only man she ever intended to be civil to again would either wear a Roman collar or a stethoscope around his neck.

Susan's bed had already been made up, and the room was stifling hot. She called the porter and with his help managed to open the window. He told her, or she thought he told her, that they would arrive in San Miguelito at six-fifteen that night. And no, he did not believe the air conditioning would be restored today. Perhaps next week.

When he went out and closed the door, Susan leaned back against the plush-covered seat, teeth clenched to keep from being ill, and watched the Mexican countryside speed by.

"September's a wonderful month in Mexico," Maria had told her. "The summer rains have gone. It's warm during the day, but the evenings are crisp and cool. You're going to love San Miguelito. It's the prettiest town in Mexico, high up in the mountains, surrounded by even higher mountain peaks. My house is way up on a hill and you can see forever. I'm so sorry I won't be there, Susie. Especially now when you need me. If there was any way I could get out of the contract in Spain I would."

"I understand, Maria. And don't worry about me. I'm going to be fine."

"I've got a maid by the name of Esperanza who comes in every day. I know she'll take good care of you." Maria had hesitated again, and then she'd asked, "What about Zachary, Susie? Does he know you're leaving?"

"There isn't any need for him to know."

Zachary Owens. Family friend, the man who'd helped her get a job with his law firm when she first came to Houston a year and a half ago. The man she'd always looked up to.

At forty-three, Zachary was attractive. Tall and well-built, hair graying at the temples, moustache neatly trimmed, he looked as though he had stepped from the pages of *Town and Country*.

When Susan moved to Houston he had taken her under his wing and decided, he said in his charmingly cultured voice, to introduce her to the finer things of life. He scoffed at her taste for country-and-western music and her once-a-week craving for pepperoni pizza.

"Pizza is out," he'd said with a tolerant smile. "Sushi is in."

She thought Zachary was the most sophisticated man she'd ever known, not at all like the young men she'd been accustomed to dating back in Granbury or at college.

Besides, Zachary was an old family friend. She'd known him since she was a child. She didn't think of their occasional dinners as dates, but as pleasurable evenings spent with a man who, though younger than her father, was her father's friend as well as hers.

They began to see each other more frequently after her father's death, and when the perfunctory kiss on the forehead changed to a not-too-demanding kiss on the lips, Susan didn't object. Zachary was comfortable; she could trust him.

When he asked her to be his date at the big company party, she accepted. Wanting to please him, she'd bought a dress that she couldn't really afford and had her hair done at Arden's.

The evening hadn't started out too well. Some of the executives had raised eyebrows when their vice president walked in with one of the junior secretaries. She hadn't liked it when Zachary introduced her as his protégé. "She's my Eliza Doolittle," he told Susan's boss. "She can almost tell an Erté from a Warhol now."

Zachary drank a great deal more than she'd ever seen him drink that night, and when they finally left the party, he'd called for a taxi. In the cab he told Susan how lovely she looked. "You're a fetching little creature with infinite potential. There are a million things I want to teach you, things much more interesting than music and art."

He'd reached for her but she'd moved farther away. Zachary had never been like this before; it made her uncomfortable.

When they arrived at her apartment, he let the cab go before she could protest. "I'm desperately in need of a cup of coffee," he'd said. "One cup and I'll be on my way."

So Susan had let him in.

And he had raped her.

Afterward he'd said, "Don't pretend you didn't like it, Susan. And don't try to make trouble for me, darling, or I'll smatter your reputation all over Houston."

Then he'd straightened his clothes and said, "I'll see you in the office tomorrow. Let's have lunch, shall we?"

She hadn't gone to the office the next day or any other day. She changed her phone number and when Zachary managed to get it and called, she hung up on him. He came to her apartment several times but Susan wouldn't answer the door. And finally he had stopped trying to see her.

She went to see him a month and a half later when she knew that she was pregnant.

"Pregnant!" He'd stared at her, white faced and angry. "How in the hell could you be so stupid? You're twenty-three years old. Weren't you on the pill?"

"There wasn't any reason to be on the pill." She clutched the edge of his desk. "I thought you should know," she said. "That's why I'm here."

"Sure it is." He opened the desk drawer and reached for his checkbook. "All right, Susan. How much? Five thousand? That should more than cover an abortion and a nice little trip to bring the color back into your cheeks. You're looking a little peaked and thin, dear. Maybe you'd better start eating pizza again."

He flung the check across the desk. She'd looked at it, then at him, and with a strangled cry she'd picked it up and torn it into a dozen pieces.

That night she'd called Maria Mendoza and said, "I'm pregnant. Can I come to Mexico?"

"But you can get an abortion in Houston, Susie."

"I don't want an abortion."

"You're kidding! You mean that after what that man did to you, you're going to keep the baby?"

"It's my baby, Maria, the only family I have now." Her voice had clogged with tears. "I can't give it up."

Never. Not for anything or anybody.

Susan leaned back against the train seat and put her hands protectively over her stomach. "My baby," she whispered. Then she closed her eyes and rocked by the swaying motion of the train, she went to sleep.

By four o'clock the heat in the train was almost unbearable, and the next time the train stopped Susan picked up her shoulder bag and stepped down to the platform.

"How long will we be here?" she asked one of the conductors.

He said something she didn't understand. Before she could ask him again he turned away to speak to another conductor, and Susan headed for the ladies' room. She looked at herself in the cracked mirror over the washstand and groaned. Her face was red and her hair looked limp and unkempt. She put her bag down and splashed cold water on her hands and face, then reached in her bag for her hairbrush and began brushing her hair. She was reaching for her lipstick when she heard the train whistle. Quickly then, she applied the lipstick and blotted it with a tissue. Only two more hours and they'd be in San Miguelito. A cold shower and a good night's sleep would help... She stopped. Train wheels were turning. Engines were chugging.

She ran out of the station, crying out in disbelief as the train sped by.

Unable to believe that it had left without her, Susan looked around. There were no taxis, no buildings except for the small empty station. The only sound was the wind blowing in dust off the dry, cactus-covered land.

"What are you doing here?"

Susan whirled to see Armando Cobian coming around the side of the building.

He raised one dark eyebrow. "I thought you were going on to San Miguelito."

"I was. I am. I just got off the train to get some air. I didn't think it would leave so quickly. I was in the ladies' room." She looked down the tracks as the train disappeared around the curve of a mountain. "All my bags are on the train," she cried. "What am I going to do?"

"There's a phone in the station. If you like I can call the station master in San Miguelito and tell him to get your luggage."

"I'd appreciate that, Mr. Cobian." Susan clutched her purse and tried to stay calm. "I wonder if you could tell me where I might get a taxi."

"There aren't any taxis, Señorita Alexander."

Susan bit her lip. "Perhaps you could call one for me. There must be a town close by."

"I'm afraid there isn't." He indicated the water tower. "This stop is mostly to take on water. A few people like me, who have ranches close by, get on and off here. But there isn't any town."

"But... but what am I going to do?"

Armando hesitated. "Look," he said. "One of my men is coming to pick me up. You'd better come out to my ranch with me for the night. In the morning I'll have someone drive you to San Miguelito."

Susan stared at him. "I couldn't possibly do that," she said stiffly. "I'll just wait for the next train. Do you know when it's due?"

The slightest of smiles curved his mouth. "The day after tomorrow, if it's on schedule."

"The day after...?" Susan's eyes widened. What was she going to do? There weren't any taxis and as far as she could see there certainly wasn't a friendly hotel or motel. There wasn't even a soft-drink stand inside the station. She looked down the narrow gravel road that led to nowhere and saw a cloud of dust moving toward them.

"That will be my man," Armando said. "I hope you'll reconsider and come with me." He searched for the words to reassure her because he knew she was frightened. He couldn't very well abandon her; he had to convince her to come with him.

"My ranch is about thirty miles from here," he said conversationally. "We'll be there in time for supper. My housekeeper, Juanita, is a wonderful cook and I know she'd like nothing better than having a guest to fuss over." He glanced over at the station. "The station master is about to lock up," he told Susan. "I'd better make that call for you before he does."

She watched him walk toward the station, say something to the uniformed man there, then disappear inside. How could she have been so stupid? Only idiots missed trains and planes. And how in heaven's name could she go riding off into the sunset with a man she didn't even know? All she knew about him was that he had a ranch and that he was a friend of Father Ramiro's.

That at least was something. It didn't necessarily make him man of the year, but on the other hand, it didn't make him Jack the Ripper, either. She felt hot tears sting her eyes. Oh, dammit, anyway, what was she going to do?

By the time Armando came back, a white pickup truck had pulled alongside the station and a moustachioed man with a wide sombrero got out.

"Buenas tardes, jefe," he said. *"¿Como esta?"*

"Bien, José. This is Señorita Alexander. She's coming out to the ranch with us." Armando opened the pickup door and to Susan said, "After you."

But still Susan hesitated. "If you could take me to a hotel—"

"The nearest hotel is in San Miguelito. That's a three-hour drive from here and an hour's drive from my ranch." Armando's voice grew serious. "You are a guest in my country," he said. "It would not be hospitable or proper for me to leave you here alone. I assure you, one of my men will drive you to San Miguelito right after breakfast in the morning."

Susan turned back to the station. It was locked and the station master had already headed across the fields in the direction of the mountains. The sun was going down; it would be dark soon. She looked up at Armando Cobian and knew she didn't have any choice. She had to go with him.

"Please," he said, and held the door open for her to enter.

Chapter Two

Through the approaching darkness Susan saw a sign that read, La Gloria. José turned off the gravel road onto a narrower road and drove for more than five minutes before she saw the sprawling white house with a red-tiled roof.

"Is La Gloria a family name?" she asked Armando.

"No, it means glory or heaven. That's what my grandfather named the ranch when he came here from Spain."

José said something in Spanish, and when Armando said *"Muy bien,"* José stopped the pickup and got out. He tipped his sombrero to Susan and with a murmured *"Buenas noches, señorita,"* he turned and disappeared into the shadows.

Armando slid behind the wheel. "I like this time of night," he said. "Everything stills and all you can hear are the night birds and the crickets." He gestured to his right. "Our horses are in the fields over there. I'll show them to you tomorrow after breakfast if you like. We've been raising them for four generations and we produce some of the finest stock in North America."

"Don't let a Texan hear you say that," Susan said with a smile as she began to relax. All during the ride here she'd remembered every horror story she'd ever heard about what happened to women who accepted rides from strangers. And even though she really hadn't had any choice about whether to sit outside of the station all night or accept Armando Cobian's hospitality, she'd felt awfully uncomfortable about getting into the pickup with him.

But he'd been a perfect gentleman. He and the man José had chatted during the drive, and occasionally Armando had turned to say something to her. He'd been very formal and correct and little by little her uncertainty had eased.

"Was your grandmother Spanish, too?" she asked.

"No, she was Mexican. Grandfather came to Mexico to buy wild horses to take back to his ranch near Granada. He wanted to mix the two breeds, the Spanish blood with the Mexican. But he met my grandmother and he stayed in Mexico. He said that he fell in love the moment he saw her."

Armando turned and smiled at Susan. "I'm not sure that I believe in love at first sight, but I know he adored her." He leaned his head against the back of the seat because he was tired and because it was pleasant to sit here for a few moments with this young American woman. The air was cooler than it had been all day. A fresh breeze blew in off the fields and he could smell clover and hay and the scent of the horses.

"This is where my father and all of his sisters were born, where I was born. My father died when I was very young and my grandfather raised me. I asked him once why he hadn't gone back to Spain, except to buy horses, and he said that his home was here where my grandmother was, and that wherever she was would always be heaven to him. That's why he named the ranch La Gloria."

"It's a lovely name."

"Yes, it is." He started the white pickup. "But you're tired and I shouldn't sit here talking." He drove toward the house and when they reached it, he pulled up in front of the circular drive and stopped before a wrought-iron gate. He got out and quickly came around to help Susan out of the truck. And when he had opened the gate, he let her inside a flower-filled patio.

She had never been in a Mexican home before and she looked around curiously. The patio was patterned tile. There was a lovely stone fountain in the center, surrounded by blooming azaleas. Ferns and other blossoming plants edged the patio, and beyond she could see the Spanish arches that led to a brightly lighted room.

"Come along." Armando took her arm. He opened the French doors and led her inside. He called, "Juanita?" and in a moment a middle-aged woman hurried into the room. Tall and broad of bust and hip, she wore a starched white blouse and a black skirt that was covered with a bright red apron. Her hair was pulled tightly away from her face and hung in one thick braid down the middle of her back.

"I've brought a guest," he said in slow, distinct English. "She is going to San Miguelito, but she got off the train for a few minutes and it left without her. She'll stay here tonight and tomorrow José or one of the other men will drive her in to San Miguelito."

"*Ay, pobrecita. ¿Y que pasa con sus maletas?*"

Armando turned to Susan. "She wants to know what happened to your suitcases." He grinned. "Juanita understands English but she's too embarrassed to speak it." And to Juanita he said, "They'll be waiting for Señorita Alexander when she gets to San Miguelito. Now, suppose you show her to one of the guest rooms and when she's ready, we'll have something to eat."

The room that Juanita took Susan to was twice the size of the bedroom she'd had in the Houston apartment. The heavy Spanish-style furniture was beautifully carved. The double bed was covered with a pale apricot spread that matched the silken drapes and the velvet chaise that stood in one corner of the room. The walls had been painted a delicate shade of yellow, and there was a small table and two chairs in front of the French doors.

The adjoining bathroom where she washed her hands and face was large and airy. She wished she had time for a shower, but she didn't want to keep Señor Cobian waiting. She didn't feel as uncertain about being here as she had before. It had been kind of him to rescue her and now that she had met Juanita, she was beginning to relax. Tomorrow she would be in San Miguelito and perhaps next week, to show her appreciation, she would invite Cobian for dinner.

The dining room table, large enough to accommodate twenty or more guests, had been set for two with colorful Mexican pottery. There was a bouquet of peonies in the center of the table and crystal wine goblets that sparkled in the light.

"Juanita wanted me to tell you that she apologizes for the poor dinner. If she'd known I was bringing a guest, she would have prepared something special." He filled Susan's glass with dark red wine. "I rarely entertain, so she cooks just for me. But I know she likes the idea of company." He touched his glass to Susan's. "*Bienvenida*, Señorita Alexander. *Mi casa es su casa*, which means welcome, my house is your house."

"Thank you, Señor Cobian. And thank you for letting me stay here." She'd had nothing to drink during her pregnancy, and now she took only a small sip of the wine. "I don't think I would have enjoyed sleeping on the steps outside the station house."

"With only the coyotes to keep you company?" He grinned. "Please call me Armando," he said. "May I call you Susana?"

"Susana? I think I like that better than Susan."

Juanita brought the "poor" dinner in then; chilled gazpacho, roast beef, fresh asparagus and a crisp garden salad. There was flan, custard with a carmelized sauce for dessert and rich dark coffee flavored with cinnamon.

Over dinner Susan learned that Armando had traveled a great deal in the United States and that he had a degree in agronomy from the University of Texas, as well as a degree in law from the University of Guanajuato in Mexico.

But she offered no information about herself and Armando was curious. She was such a delicately made young woman, of medium height, and so slim she seemed almost fragile. She was dressed simply, but in good taste, in a light blue suit and high-heeled matching sandals. Her face was porcelain pale and in the glow of candlelight her amber eyes looked large and luminous.

It suddenly struck Armando that it had been a very long time since he'd had dinner with anyone as beautiful and desirable as this young American and that he thoroughly enjoyed being with her.

She wasn't a chatterer, but when she spoke her voice was rich and softly modulated. She told Juanita, in carefully worded English, how delicious everything had been and thanked her for the dinner.

He wanted to ask her why she had come to Mexico alone and why she was going to live in San Miguelito. Had she had a broken love affair? Was that why she sometimes looked so sad? Or had it been the loss of her father that brought that strangely lost and waiflike look to her eyes?

He decided that he would drive her to San Miguelito in the morning himself and see that she was safely settled in. And that he would ask her to dinner in a day or two.

When Juanita came in to clear the dishes, Armando said, "Perhaps you'd like to rest now, Susana."

"Yes." She brushed the heavy chestnut hair back off her neck and he had a sudden strong desire to put his hand around that slender white column and draw her close. But then she offered her hand and said, "Thank you, Mr. Cobian . . . Armando. I don't know what I would have done if you hadn't rescued me."

Her hand felt small and warm in his. One tug, he thought, and she would be in his arms.

"I'm glad I was there," he said politely. "If you need anything don't hesitate to ask Juanita. Sleep as late as you like in the morning. We're only an hour's drive from San Miguelito so there's no great hurry to get going. I'll show you around the ranch after you've had breakfast."

"I'd like that." She hesitated. "Good night," she said, and turned to follow the waiting Juanita out of the room.

Armando went back to the table. He started to pick up his glass of wine, but instead he picked up Susan's glass. He took a sip from it, then slowly ran the rim of it back and forth against his lips.

Susana, he thought. And drank the wine.

She awoke sometime during the night and knew that she was ill. By morning she was burning with fever and so weak she couldn't hold her head up. At eight-thirty Juanita knocked and came into the room with a breakfast tray. When she saw Susan she said, *"Ay, pobrecita. ¿Que pasa?"*

She felt Susan's head. "Doctor," she said. "You must have a doctor."

"No, I'll be all right. If I just rest a little longer—"

"No, no. You are very sick. I must tell Señor Cobian." And before Susan could stop her, Juanita hurried out of the room.

Susan closed her eyes, willing her stomach to right itself and the bed to stop rocking. But she opened them when Armando said, "Susana? What is it? Are you ill?"

She felt his cool hand on her forehead. "Sorry about this," she whispered.

"I phoned my doctor. He'll be here in a little while. Is there anything you'd like? A glass of water?"

"No, thank you."

"How long have you been ill?"

"Since about midnight."

"You should have called Juanita. Or me. You're probably dehydrated by now. Sure you don't want any water?"

"I couldn't keep it down."

"All right then. Close your eyes. I'll stay with you."

Susan wanted to protest, but she felt too awful to say anything. She barely knew Armando, yet it was so reassuring to have him here beside her.

When the doctor came, Armando left the room. No wonder she'd looked so pale last night, and yesterday on the train, he thought, and why now her face was as white as the old-fashioned cotton gown Juanita had given her to wear. She looked very young and defenseless. She was alone, a stranger in a strange country and he couldn't help feeling an overwhelming need to protect her.

"I don't think it's anything too serious," the doctor said when he came out of the room. "It's probably a combination of things—the heat, a change in the water, different food and perhaps stress. I've given her something for the nausea and I've left pills with Juanita. She'll sleep for a while now, but when she awakens, be sure she takes the pills and that she drinks as much liquid as possible." He snapped his bag shut. "Friend of yours?" he asked.

"Not really. I met her on the train yesterday. She got off at Estancia Grande to get some air and the train left without her. She was stranded so I brought her here for the night."

"I'm afraid she's going to be here longer than that. I should say she'll be in bed for at least a week. You could have her sent to the hospital in San Miguelito, of course."

"No, she can stay here. Juanita will take care of her."

"Good." The doctor started toward the door. "I'll phone later to see how she is. And I'll see her in the morning."

A week or more, Armando thought when the doctor left. He wasn't sure how he felt about that. He rarely had guests here at the ranch, and except for his Aunt Inocencia and Sophia, he never had female guests. But he wouldn't hear of Susan's going to a hospital. Juanita would take care of her, and he'd look in on her—once in a while, at least.

He was there every time Susan opened her eyes. He raised her head and held water or cool fresh orange juice to her lips. "Here, muchacha, drink this," he always said, and the hands that lifted her head to drink were tender.

By the end of the week she felt strong enough to get out of bed. Armando had sent one of his men to San Miguelito to pick up her two suitcases, and when she had showered and washed her hair, she put on one of her own gowns and the matching robe.

She was lying on the chaise in front of the open French doors when Armando knocked and came in.

"Juanita told me you were feeling better," he said. "You've had a rough time."

"I've been a total nuisance." Susan shook her head. "I bet this is the last time you'll ever rescue a stranded female. You should have left me for the coyotes."

"They wouldn't have appreciated you."

A smile tugged at the corners of her lips, then she sobered. "This has been a terrible imposition, Armando. I can't thank you and Juanita enough for what you've done for me, but I do thank you, with all my heart. I'm all right, now. I'll be ready to leave tomorrow if one of your men can drive me to San Miguelito."

"Not tomorrow," he said firmly. "And not the day after. You're still very weak. Besides—" he smiled "—I want a chance to show you around the ranch."

"Armando, I can't impose. I—"

"You're not imposing." He took her hand. "I want you to stay until you're completely well, Susana. Besides, if I let you go too soon, I'm afraid Juanita will go with you."

"She's wonderful."

"Yes, she is. I couldn't do without her, so please don't think of going until you're completely well." He squeezed her hand. "All right."

"Muy bien." She smiled. "Juanita's been teaching me Spanish."

"And you've got her speaking a few words of English. That's because she likes you."

I like you, too, he almost added. And he'd liked having her here. Though still pale and peaked, she looked very pretty this morning in her light blue gown and matching lacy robe.

"My grandmother decorated this room," he said. "She said that women like soft colors and that every woman should have a chaise to make her feel special and romantic."

"It's something I've always wanted and never had. Your grandmother was right, it does make a woman feel special."

"And romantic?" He was sorry as soon as he'd said the words because she drew her hand from his and her face became as guarded as it had been when he first met her. He stood up and wanting to change the subject, said, "Is there anyone who should know where you are? A friend or..." He hesitated. "Someone who might be worried about you?"

"There's no one."

So there wasn't any special man in her life. That pleased him, but he didn't know why it did.

Susan felt strong enough on the following night to dress, and because the night was soft and warm, Juanita served dinner out on the patio.

Once again Susan said, "I'm all right now. I can leave tomorrow."

And again Armando said, "No, not tomorrow. I want to show you around the ranch tomorrow. Perhaps the day after." He smiled at her. "I've gotten rather used to having you here, Susana. I don't want you to leave."

"I've been nothing but a bother and a nuisance from the moment we met. I should think you'd be glad to be rid of me."

"Maybe I've been lonelier than I realized."

"Don't you ever have guests?"

"My Aunt Inocencia comes to visit occasionally. She and her mother live in Comonfort. That's not too far from here. She's a *soltera*, a single woman, somewhere in her middle sixties. I think you'd like her."

"She's never been married?"

Armando shook his head.

"And she still lives with her mother?"

He looked surprised. "Of course. That's the way it should be. A woman's place is with her family until she is married."

"No matter how old she is?"

"Age has nothing to do with it."

"Has she ever had a boyfriend?"

"Years ago. His name is Francisco Gutierez. He and Inocencia have been friends for the last forty years, in spite of her family's objections."

"Why does her family object?"

"Francisco is a divorced man."

"How long has he been divorced?"

"Almost forty years. He married when he was a young man but the marriage didn't last."

Susan's eyes widened. "He's been divorced for forty years?"

Armando nodded. "So of course her family would not permit the marriage."

"But the woman's in her sixties!" Susan said unbelievingly.

"She is still under her mother's care." He shrugged. "Perhaps when Doña Sophia dies, Inocencia will marry Francisco. But certainly not before."

"That's terrible!"

"We have our customs," he said stiffly. "Things have changed in cities like Mexico City and Guadalajara, but here in the provinces people tend to stick to the old ways." He looked up as Juanita appeared and began serving their dinner. "There are proper ways of doing things and we are still very proper, very traditional people."

Susan looked down at her chicken consommé, the words *we are proper, traditional people,* echoing in her mind. What would Armando say if he knew she was pregnant? What would he think of her then?

When they had finished dinner, Armando asked her if she was tired. And when she said that she wasn't, he suggested a walk.

"I'd like to show you the stables," he said. "I have a new foal I should check on." He got up and pulled her chair out.

There were a dozen mares in the stable, along with the three-day-old foal. He was shiny and brown with a streak of white on his nose.

"Oh, you beauty," Susan said when he nuzzled her hand for the piece of sugar Armando had given her. "Aren't you gorgeous."

"He's a fifth generation, from the same bloodline my grandfather started when he bought the ranch back in the early 1900s. His father's name is Sultan."

Susan scratched the foal's ears. "Maybe that makes you a maharaja," she said.

"Or Raja." Armando smiled at her. "I think you've just named him."

"Really?" She looked inordinately pleased.

"Really." He ran a hand over the foal's flanks. "Now you'll have a reason to come back. You've named him, so he's partly yours. It's only right that you should visit him."

Her lips curved in a smile and suddenly he knew that he wanted to kiss her. In an off-the-shoulder blue dress, her perfumed shoulders were creamy white. He looked at the pale, delicate hands stroking the colt, and his body tightened with the thought of how her hands would feel stroking him. He gripped the top wooden bar of the stall and took a deep breath.

"Tell me about your grandfather." Susan smiled up at him. "What kind of a man was he?"

"He could be tough and demanding," Armando said after a moment or two. "But never with the people he loved. He cleared the land and built the ranch from nothing. My grandmother's parents wouldn't let her marry him until he'd built the house, but on the day it was finished he carried her across the threshold as his bride."

"And their marriage was happy?"

Armando nodded. "Happy and special," he said. "I remember once, when my grandparents were in their late seventies or early eighties, I came upon them here in the stable. They were kissing, as passionately as young lovers. My grandfather had his hand on grandmother's breast and I heard him say, 'It will never change, Sarah. As long as I have a breath left in my body, I'll feel this way about you.' And she said, 'When I die, yours will be the last name I say and I will carry your dear face with me when I cross onto the other side.'"

Armando shook his head. "I don't know why I told you that," he said in a voice made rough by all that he was feeling. "I've never told anybody..." He stopped, for tears, like tiny drops of crystal, clung to her eyelashes.

"Susana?" he whispered, and very gently he wiped her tears away with his fingertips. Then, because he could not help himself, he kissed her.

Her mouth trembled under his and he felt her soft gasp of surprise. He put his arms around her and her lips softened, but only for a moment. When she stepped away from him she said, "A love like that must be very rare. I don't suppose they're still alive?"

"No." Armando let his arms fall to his sides. "Grandmother went first, grandfather died a week later." He reached for Susan's hands. "Are you sorry I kissed you?"

"I...I don't know." Her amber eyes were troubled. "But I think we should go back to the house."

"All right."

She bent to touch the foal's head and whispered, "Good night, Raja. I'll see you tomorrow."

As he watched her, Armando wanted, more than he had ever wanted anything in his life, to take her in his arms and hold her for a very long time. He wanted to stroke her chestnut hair, to feel the whole lovely, feminine length of her body against his. He wanted to lay her down on the sweet-smelling straw and kiss her until both of them went a little crazy. He wanted . . .

Instead he took her hand and led her out of the stable.

Chapter Three

The hills were alive with autumn colors. Fields of wild poppies colored the landscape. Lupine and mountain laurel grew at random on the rugged slopes.

Armando reined in his horse. "You can see the ranch from here," he said. "There, over to your left."

Susan looked down upon fields made golden in the morning sun. In the distance she could see the house nestled amid a stand of poplars. Beyond were the stable, the corral and the pastures where dozens of horses grazed.

"It's a lovely setting," she said, glad now that she had stayed this extra day so that Armando could show her the ranch.

They had ridden first around the perimeter of his property, pausing at green pasturelands where Arabians and Andalusian mares, their colts and fine strong stallions roamed free.

It had been a long time since she'd been on a horse, but Armando had set a slow pace and she hadn't had any problem keeping up, even when they'd climbed up into the hills.

Tomorrow he would drive her to San Miguelito, and while she was anxious to settle into Maria's house, she was strangely reluctant to leave the ranch. And him.

She had only known Armando Cobian for a week. He had been kind to her while she'd been ill. Except for that one brief kiss, he'd behaved like a perfect gentleman. Too perfect? She repressed a smile and said a silent, shame on you. What do you want him to do? Sweep you into his arms and kiss the stuffing out of you?

And a part of her thought, hmm, maybe I do.

"You can see the village of Comonfort from here," Armando said, breaking in on her thoughts. "There's the church steeple. That's where Aunt Inocencia goes to Sunday Mass. She sees Francisco there, and afterward he takes her home."

"That's it?"

"That's it. Anything else would be unacceptable."

"And you approve of an arrangement like that?"

"It isn't up to me to approve or disapprove. As far as her family is concerned, it's the correct thing to do."

"But you said that her father is dead. There's only her mother."

"And six brothers. The eldest is the head of the family now that their father is dead."

"But the poor woman's life is passing her by. She could have had a husband and children, but all she has is an hour or two every Sunday in church. That's terrible!"

"We're an old-fashioned Catholic people, Susana. Certain things are not permitted. Inocencia could have run away and married Francisco, but she chose to obey her family."

"I still think it's terrible," Susan said, angry enough now to bite him on his kneecap. "If her family loved her, they'd want her to be happy."

"I assure you, Inocencia is quite happy the way she is." Armando had been frowning, but now the frown faded and he said, "I'll introduce you to her and let you see for yourself that she's quite content with her life. Why don't I invite her for dinner some Sunday? I'll go to San Miguelito for you and then we'll pick up Inocencia and her mother."

"And Francisco?"

He shook his head. "No, of course not." He motioned his horse forward, ending the conversation.

Fifteen minutes later he reined his mount in under a stand of pine trees. "Let's have lunch here," he said, and when he dismounted he helped Susan down. They spread a blanket under the trees, then unpacked the lunch that Juanita had prepared. There was chicken and ham, two kinds of cheese, tomatoes and radishes, fresh-baked bread and strawberry tarts.

"Do you think we'll have enough to eat?" Armando said with a laugh. "The way Juanita cooks, it's a wonder I don't weigh three hundred pounds. As it is, I put on a few pounds that I didn't need the last month or two. I've got to start being careful."

"But you're perfect just the way you are," Susan protested. "You've got a marvelous build. Nice broad shoulders, narrow waist and hips..." She stopped, blushing. "I mean...I mean I think you're...uh, fine just the way you are."

"I'll remember you said that when I take an extra tart," Armando said with a grin. "Juanita is going to hate to see you leave tomorrow. She's enjoyed having a woman to fuss over." He handed her a plate. "Will you have help in San Miguelito?"

Susan nodded. "Maria has someone who comes in every day. She's probably wondering when I'm going to arrive." She reached for a chicken leg. "I don't know how good a cook she is, but I hope you'll come for dinner sometime."

"You name the date and I'll be there." Armando hesitated, then unable to help himself he said, "It's hard for me to believe there isn't anyone special in your life, Susana. That there's no one waiting for you back in Texas."

Susan looked down at her plate. "There's no one," she said. "There was someone in college that I liked, but we broke up just before he graduated."

"Then there's certainly something wrong with all the men in Texas. Mexican men would have more sense than to let somebody as pretty as you run loose." He passed her the home-baked bread. Looking suddenly very serious, he said, "I'd like to see you again, Susan. After you leave here, I mean."

Susan looked at him, then away. Tell him you're pregnant, a voice inside her head warned. Tell him now. Swallowing hard she said, "Armando, there's something..." She stopped. It was too soon. She tried to smile but her face felt stiff. "Of—of course," she managed to say. "I've already invited you to dinner, haven't I?"

A slight frown puckered the space between his eyebrows because it wasn't the answer he had hoped for. But it would do for now. He wanted to see her as often as he could because he liked her freshness, her sweet air of innocence. Her innocence. That excited him, and looking at her now he thought how exciting it would be to teach Susana the ways of love, to awaken her to passion and have her respond to him.

After they had eaten and cleared away what was left from the lunch, he stretched out on the blanket. "How about a siesta before we start back?" he asked with a yawn.

"I'm not sleepy." Susan tried unsuccessfully to smother a yawn. "That wasn't fair," she said when he laughed. "That was only a copycat yawn, an involuntary response."

Armando patted the space next to him. "C'mon," he said. "I'm too sleepy to bite."

Susan lay down, two feet from him, her body tense, rigid, ready to fight him off. She waited. He didn't move, so she darted a look at him. His eyes were closed, his breathing even, his full curved lips slightly parted.

He was different from anybody she'd ever met. His face was thin and almost aesthetically classic. His eyes were ever so slightly tilted. He had high cheekbones, a straight nose and just the hint of a cleft in his chin. The hands that lay crossed over his chest were strong and finely boned. His fingers were long and slender, the nails short and clean.

Susan's gaze moved down his body. His blue-checked shirt, open at the throat, gave her a glimpse of curly chest hair. Tailor-made blue jeans snugged tight over his flat stomach and narrow hips. His long, well-shaped legs looked muscled and strong. Suddenly and unexpectedly a flame ignited somewhere in Susan's midsection. She clamped her teeth hard against her lower lip as she turned away and closed her eyes.

But still she saw Armando, the whole long masculine length of him, lying so close. All she had to do was reach out her hand . . .

Susan willed herself to breathe slowly, evenly, and at last, although she was sure she wouldn't, she went to sleep.

When she awoke, Armando was leaning on his elbow, watching her. "It's time to head back to the ranch," he said gently. "Juanita's preparing a special dinner for your last night with us. She'll be upset if I don't get you back in time to rest before we eat."

"Then we'd better go."

"Yes." But he didn't move.

Still in that place of half sleeping, half waking, Susan looked up at him, held by the expression in his Spanish-green eyes. She knew she should move but a strange lethargy kept her still, waiting . . . waiting until he said, "Susana?" and leaned to kiss her.

It was a tender, questing kiss. Susan brought her hands up to push him away, but instead, she flattened them against his chest. His breath was sweet, his mouth so tender that without conscious thought her lips parted under his. And when she felt the tip of his tongue against her lips, the same fire she'd felt when she'd watched him sleeping kindled and grew.

The kiss lengthened and the world narrowed to this tiny space of time. Susan could feel the beat of his heart beneath her palm. And because she had such a need to touch him, she opened the top buttons of his shirt and slipped her hand inside. His skin was hot from the sun, and when she splayed her fingers through the thatch of chest hair, he sighed against her lips.

As though from a distance she heard the song of the birds above them. She smelled the pine needles and the autumn grass and knew she should pull away. But, oh, there was such a need to be held by him, to be close and protected here in the shelter of his arms.

"Susana," Armando whispered against her lips. *"Mi querida*, Susana." He looked into her eyes. "All day I have wanted to kiss you like this." He kissed her closed eyelids, her nose and her cheeks. "So sweet," he murmured. "So innocent."

"Armando, I—"

But he stilled her words with a kiss and when her lips trembled under his, he eased past them to touch the tip of his tongue to hers, touched and retreated, touched and retreated, and each time he did, the fire deep within her grew brighter, hotter. And at last, because she knew she had to, she gently pushed him away.

"No more," she whispered. "Please, Armando. No more."

She felt the hesitation, the terrible tautness in his body. But he said, *"Muy bien*, Susana." He kissed her cheek and held her cradled in his arms until the tension between them eased.

Then he let her go and they mounted their horses and started the winding path down from the hills.

The moon came out, full and fat and yellow, casting light on the patio already illuminated by hanging lanterns and candlelight. The music from the stereo inside drifted outside and night-blooming jasmine scented the air.

Susan wore a white off-the-shoulder blouse with a long full skirt in a deep shade of green. Behind her ear she pinned the gardenia that Juanita had delivered to her room while she was dressing.

"Señor Cobian waits in the patio," Juanita said in her careful English when she handed the flower to Susan.

Susan smiled at herself in the mirror when Juanita left. Armando, she thought, remembering how tenderly he had kissed her today. Then her smile faded. "You've got to tell him," she said to her reflection in the mirror. "Tonight. Tell him tonight."

He looked up when she came into the patio and held his hands out to her. "You look lovely," he said. And she was glad she'd worn something special, because he, too, had dressed for the occasion in a white dinner jacket and dark trousers.

"Would you like an aperitif before dinner?" he asked.

Susan hesitated. Because of her pregnancy she wasn't drinking, but because she wanted to put off telling him, she said, "Just a little, please."

He poured a dry Spanish sherry in two small glasses and handed one to her. "Let us drink to your quick return to Rancho La Gloria," he said,

She raised the glass to her lips. I'll tell him about the baby tonight, she promised herself. And knew that when she did, whatever might be beginning between them would end.

Susan barely touched her food, and when Armando asked if she wasn't feeling well, she said, "I'm fine. I ate too much at lunch, that's all."

He looked across the table at her. Reaching for her hand he said, "I've grown accustomed to having you here, Susana. I hate to see you leave tomorrow."

"And I hate to leave, Armando. I can't even begin to tell you what your kindness has meant to me. There's no way I can ever thank you."

"You can thank me by staying awhile longer."

Susan shook her head. "I can't," she said.

"We'll see each other often."

She hesitated for the fraction of a second before she murmured, "Yes, of course."

He put his fork down. "Come and dance with me," he said.

Almost reluctantly Susan let him help her up and lead her over near the stone fountain. There was a Mexican waltz on the stereo. "They're playing *'Cuando Escuches Este Vals,'* 'When You Hear This Waltz,'" Armando told her. "The next line is, 'Remember me, the kisses you gave to me, and I gave to you.'" He kissed the top of Susan's head. "When you're in San Miguelito, think of me, Susana."

She lowered her lids so that he wouldn't see the tears that threatened to form. I'll always think of you, she wanted to tell him. Whenever I hear a waltz, when the scent of jasmine or gardenia or pine drifts on the night air. I'll think of you when the moon is as full as it is tonight. And whenever I hear the soft, sibilant sound of Spanish or the music of a guitar. She leaned her face against his shoulder and wanted this night to last forever.

Juanita came to clear the table. She asked, "Is there anything else, Señor Cobian?"

They stopped dancing long enough for Armando to say, *"Nada,* Juanita, *gracias. Hasta mañana."*

"Hasta mañana, Señor Cobian. *Hasta mañana, señorita."*

"Hasta mañana, Juanita."

"She likes you," Armando said when Juanita went inside. "She's going to miss you."

"I'm going to miss her."

"Then stay." He stopped dancing and with a finger under Susan's chin, lifted her face to his. "I've gotten so used to your being here, Susana, to seeing you across from me at breakfast and at dinner. Whatever shall I do without you?"

"You barely know me, Armando. You—"

"I know everything I need to know." He kissed her and when his arms tightened around her, she felt the warm length of his body against hers.

The kiss deepened and grew. She said, "Armando, don't, please—"

"Querida," he whispered against her lips. *"Mi preciosa*, Susana." He kissed her again, deeply, urgently. He tightened his arms around her and put one hand against the small of her back to press her closer.

She felt his arousal. With a gasp she tried to move away, for suddenly she was afraid, as afraid as she'd been that terrible night in her apartment. Armando wanted her the same way Zachary had wanted her. She had to stop him before he did what Zachary had done.

The memory of what had happened made her throat close in fear. There'd been no warning, no preliminaries. Zachary had grabbed her and held her against him, the way Armando held her now. He'd pressed wet kisses on her mouth and when she'd struggled he'd said, "You want it. You know you want it."

She'd tried to break away but he'd followed her. She'd felt the back of the sofa behind her knees, and though she'd struggled, Zachary had pushed her backward until she fell. He lay on top of her, pinning her with his body while he pressed open-mouth kisses against her lips, her throat, her breasts. He ripped her dress and when she fought him, he grasped her wrists. And though she had screamed and fought and pleaded, he had taken her, ruthlessly, violently.

With a cry she pushed Armando away. "Don't!" she begged. "Let me go!"

"Susana?" Armando stared at her. "What is it, *querida*? What's the matter?"

Amber eyes wide with fear, Susan backed away. Her body was tense, rigid, her arms crossed over her chest as though to defend herself.

"Susana, please. If I have offended you, I'm sorry." He indicated the stone fountain. "Come," he said, "let's sit down."

Susan stared at him, and as quickly as it had come, the fear left her body. Her arms dropped to her sides. She took a deep shaking breath. "I'm . . . I'm sorry. I suddenly realized how alone we were. That frightened me."

"Do you think I would ever hurt you, Susana? That I would ever do anything against your will? Don't you know that I'm beginning to care for you? That when you leave here I want to continue to see you?" Armando brought her hand to his lips.

"I hate the idea of your living alone in San Miguelito," he said. "If you would permit me, I will speak to my Aunt Inocencia and her mother. They have a large house. You can move in with them. You would be safe and cared for there. I could see you often . . ." He hesitated, and then with a smile said, "I'm being too presumptuous, aren't I? I don't mean to be, Susana, but I hate the idea of your living alone without the proper protection, even from me." He brushed a lock of hair back off her face. "Don't be afraid of me, Susana," he said. "I'll never hurt you. I'll never do anything you don't want me to do."

Susan leaned her head against his chest, and when he put his arms around her she didn't pull away. Nor did she struggle when he put a finger under her chin and lifted her face to his and very gently kissed her. Then he held her, one hand against the back of her head, and said, "Something is happening between us, Susana. I'm not sure I believe, as my grandfather did, in love at first sight. I only know the thought of never seeing you again terrifies me."

"Armando..." Susan's throat worked with the need to cry. "We don't know anything about each other," she managed to say.

The moment was here, she had to tell him.

"I know all that I need to know."

"Please..." She stepped away from him. Hands pressed close to her sides, steeling herself, she said, "There's something I have to tell you. Something I should have told you before this."

"What is it, Susana?" Armando smiled. "Are you hiding a husband back in Texas? Do you have a secret lover? What is it, my dear?"

Susan looked up at him and knew she would have given her soul not to say the words that had to be said. She wanted him to hold her again. She wanted to lean against him and feel the strength of his arms around her.

"Armando, I—I'm pregnant."

He stared at her. His arms dropped to his sides and his face went cold and still.

Susan swallowed hard. "I'm sorry, Armando. I should have told you before." She took a deep, shaking breath. "I'm almost three-months pregnant."

The color drained from his face. "Who...who is the father? Where is he?"

"In Houston."

"Are you going to marry him?"

"No."

"Why not? If he is the father..." His features hardened. "Or perhaps you're not sure who the father is."

Susan flinched and turned away. "I didn't deserve that," she whispered.

"Didn't you?"

The music of another waltz drifted out from the living room. The candles on the table flickered and died. A cloud slipped silently across the moon.

"You were right," he said, and stood up. "We don't know anything about each other."

"I'm so sorry."

"There's no need to be. What I said before was precipitous. You're a very beautiful young woman and—"

"Please." Susan held up one pale hand as though to shield herself. "I'll be ready to leave in the morning."

Armando nodded. "I'll have José drive you in."

José. Not himself.

Susan nodded. "Thank you for everything, Armando. You've been..." Her throat tightened with pain. "You've been very kind."

"There's no need to thank me." He didn't look at her. "Will nine o'clock be too early?"

"No. I'll be ready." She started across the patio, then she paused and said, "Good night, Armando."

"Good night, Susan."

Susan, she thought. Not Susana.

Chapter Four

All night Armando had paced his room with her words, "I'm pregnant," racing round and round inside his skull.

What a fool he'd been to think she was so sweet, so innocent. Innocent! My God, how could he have been so stupid?

As stupid as he'd been six years ago when he'd asked Mercedes Lambari to marry him. A month before the wedding he had found out that she'd had an affair the year before with a young man from Guadalajara, and he'd broken off the engagement.

"But that was before I'd met you," she'd protested. "It hasn't anything to do with you and me."

"I'm sorry," he'd said. "But it has everything to do with us. You're not what I expected you to be."

"A virgin?" Her dark eyes had widened. "Is that what you mean? Are *you* a virgin?"

"Of course not. But that's different."

"Is it?" Mercedes had shaken her head. "You're living in another century," she'd said sadly. "If I weren't so angry I'd feel sorry for you."

A year later she had married a friend of his and now she had three children, two boys and a girl.

He wasn't proud of the way he had behaved with Mercedes, but he was glad that he hadn't married her because in the year he had courted her, he had never felt about her the way he felt about Susana. No woman had ever excited him the way Susana had. Nor had he ever wanted a woman as much as he had wanted her or in the way he had wanted her. From the very beginning he'd felt such an urge to protect her, to take care of her because she had seemed so vulnerable, so innocent.

Innocent! God, what a fool he'd been. Armando closed his eyes against the pain of it. Who had the man been? What had he been like? Had Susana loved him? Did she still love him? The thought of another man touching her made the sickness of anger rise like bitter bile in his throat.

He told himself again and again during that long night that he'd only known her for a week and that he would forget her.

He left the ranch early the next morning because he didn't want to be there when Susana left. At nine o'clock he rode to the crest of a hill and watched José drive up in front of the house. Susana and Juanita came out. Juanita embraced her, and when Susana got in the pickup, he saw Juanita lift her apron to her eyes and knew that she was crying.

He watched until the pickup disappeared around a stand of trees. And felt a chill of aloneness that he had never known before.

* * *

Esperanza Sauto, a slim, dark-skinned woman with soft brown eyes and one of the nicest smiles that Susan had ever seen, was sweeping the patio when Susan arrived. She smiled shyly, shook Susan's hand and very carefully said, "No speak English."

And I no speak Spanish. Susan groaned inwardly and wondered how in the world she was going to communicate with Esperanza. She decided then that tomorrow morning she would enroll in the Spanish school that Maria had told her about. If she was going to be here for almost a year she had to learn to speak the language.

Maria's house was, as she had said, on top of a hill overlooking all of San Miguelito and the mountains beyond. The patio, although not as big as Armando's, was filled with plants and flowers. The spacious living room had windows on three sides. Bookcases lined one wall, and some of Maria's paintings, bright, colorful Mexican scenes, adorned the other walls.

A heavy Mexican sofa, done in soft colors of Mexican rose, tan and beige, and two large matching chairs, faced a huge stone fireplace. A braided carpet covered part of the tile floor. There was one bedroom with a double bed, a dresser and a nightstand, and a smaller bedroom that Maria had apparently used as a studio.

The day after she arrived, Susan walked into town. The street that she lived on was very steep, with large, uneven cobblestones that made walking difficult. But when the street leveled off near town the walking became easier.

It took her over half an hour to reach the town and when she did, she found the address of the Spanish school. She enrolled and was told she could begin the morning class the following day. That done she walked around the town, poking her nose in small curio shops, *farmacias*, straw-hat stores and pottery shops.

When Susan came to the plaza, the town square, she sat on one of the green iron benches facing a spired Gothic church. For a while she watched the shoeshine boys and the small chewing gum sellers, then she bought an English-language newspaper from Mexico City.

When the bells in the church rang the hour of noon she got up and went to a small supermarket she had passed earlier. She stocked up on groceries, then found a cab near the plaza to take her back up to Maria's house.

And through everything she did that day, Susan tried not to think about Armando.

She hadn't looked back when the pickup drove away from the house, nor had she let herself cry, as Juanita had cried when she left.

All through the long and sleepless night she had told herself that she had only known Armando for a week. It didn't matter what he thought. Just because they had kissed a few times... Susan closed her eyes. The memory of those kisses crowded out every other thought. She remembered the feel of his lips on hers, the strength of the arms that held her so close. It seemed to her she could still feel the beat of his heart under her palm, that her nostrils were still filled with his special scent.

But it was over and there was nothing she could do about it.

They were different people from different backgrounds. His was the world where maiden aunts, regardless of their age, obeyed their parents. Poor Inocencia, in love with a man named Francisco, lived alone with her aging mother because Francisco had once been married and divorced. She hadn't had the courage to live her own life because she had been raised to do the right thing, the proper thing. As Armando had. Women were virgins until they married, and if they never married they would go to their graves as pure as the day they were born.

The days passed slowly. Esperanza came every weekday morning before Susan left for her class. When Susan returned to the house on the hill, the *comida*, the large midday meal, would be ready, and after she had eaten, Esperanza would clear the dishes and leave. Susan would study Spanish and work on the next day's lesson. At night she read or listened to the radio until she fell asleep.

And tried not to think about Armando.

One day on her way back from school, she passed a small boy struggling down the hill with a cardboard box filled with kittens. As he came abreast of her he said, "Excuse me, *señorita*. Would you like to buy a kitten?"

Susan smiled down at the four squirming bundles of orange-and-white fur. *"No, gracias,"* she said.

"My mother won't permit me to keep them. I'm going to the market to try to sell them, but if I don't—" His lower lip trembled. He set the box down on the cobblestones and swiped at his nose with the back of his hand.

"I'm sorry," Susan said. "But really I can't..." One of the kittens climbed up the side of the box and spilled out onto the cobblestones. Susan picked it up and when she did she made the mistake of scratching its head. The kitten looked up at her. It blinked its yellow eyes and meowed.

"Oh, dammit," Susan murmured, and handed the boy two thousand pesos.

She named the kitten Smooch and now at night she did her lessons with Smooch curled up on the chair beside her.

At the end of her second week in San Miguelito, Susan ran into Father Ramiro. She was in the bakery, buying fresh *bolillos*, the French-bread type of roll that is a Mexican staple, and as she turned to go out she ran, quite literally, into the priest.

He said, *"Perdóname,"* and when he saw that it was Susan he laughed his great big bear of a laugh and said, "We must stop meeting like this. If you're not in a hurry, let's have a cup of coffee."

And when Susan said she'd like that, he led her across the square to a restaurant that overlooked the plaza.

"What happened to you?" he asked when their *café con leche* and sweet rolls came. "You told me you were going to San Miguelito but when the train arrived you didn't get off."

"I got off at the stop before." Susan made a face. "It was so warm inside the train that when it stopped I got off to get some fresh air. I went into the ladies' room and when I came out, the train was leaving." She shook her head. "It was a stupid thing to do."

"But there is nothing there, only the water tower. That's where my friend Armando gets off because it's the closest stop to his ranch. Did you see him?"

"Yes, he... he was kind enough to take me to his ranch. He was going to have one of his men drive me to San Miguelito the next morning, but I became ill during the night. I couldn't leave."

"Ah, yes. I remember that you didn't feel well on the train. Are you better now?"

"Yes, I'm fine, thank you. But I stayed at Mr. Cobian's ranch for over a week. He and Juanita, the woman who works for him, were very kind to me."

"Armando is a kind man," Father Ramiro said with a smile. "We've been friends since we were boys and I'm very fond of him." He put another teaspoon of sugar in his coffee. "Have you seen him since you've been here?"

"No." Susan looked down at the table. "No," she said again. And when she saw that Father Ramiro's eyebrows had drawn up together in a puzzled frown, she said, "I'm sure he's very busy."

They chatted for a little while and finally the priest said, "I must be getting along. I have a baptism in a few minutes." He smiled at Susan. "I don't know whether or not you're Catholic, Miss Alexander, so I won't say that I'll see you Sunday in church. But you're most welcome to come."

"Thank you, Father Ramiro."

"When you see Armando, will you please tell him to stop by and say hello."

"Yes, of course," she said, even though she knew she wouldn't be seeing Armando.

But Susan was wrong. She had been in town for a little over two weeks when he came.

It was a Saturday morning and Susan was in the patio watering the plants and watching Smooch chase a yellow butterfly when she heard a car stop outside her gate. When she saw the white pickup the breath caught in her throat.

Armando came in through the gate. He hesitated there, then said, "May I come in?"

Susan put the watering can down beside a flowering azalea plant. "Of course." She wiped her hands off on her jeans. "Please do."

"I had to come to San Miguelito on business." He took off his wide-brimmed straw hat. "I just happened to be passing and I thought I'd stop and see if you were all right."

Susan nodded. "I'm all right."

Armando looked around. "It's very nice here, and the view is wonderful. But it's pretty far from town, isn't it?"

"Just a little more than a mile."

"But you don't have a car."

"I like the exercise. If I'm tired or carrying groceries when I return, I take a taxi back."

He scowled. "But you shouldn't be here alone. What if something happened to you? I mean in your... your condition."

"Nothing is going to happen to me. Besides, I have a phone."

"Have you seen a doctor?"

She nodded. "Maria's doctor. He's head of the clinic, the hospital, here."

"It *is* just a clinic. If you're determined to stay in Mexico, you'd be better off in a place like Mexico City or Guadalajara."

"But I like San Miguelito." Susan ran her hands down the sides of her jeans and indicating a chair said, "Please sit down, Armando. I was about to have a cup of coffee. Won't you join me?"

He hesitated again. He felt awkward and uncertain and he told himself he shouldn't have come, that he had no business being here. And he wondered why he hadn't noticed before how Susan's hair turned red in the sunlight.

"Yes, all right," he said at last. "Thank you."

"I'll only be a minute."

When Susan reached the kitchen she leaned her fore-head against the cool refrigerator door and took a cou-ple of deep breaths. Armando was here! He'd come to make sure that she was all right.

Because he's a gentleman, she told herself. Whatever it was that had started between you isn't there anymore. He's come as a friend. That's all.

She fixed a tray with two mugs and a clay *jarro* of coffee and carried it out to the patio. Armando took the tray from her and put it on the table under the bright blue-and-white umbrella before he pulled out one of the chairs so Susan could sit down.

"How is Juanita?" she asked when she had poured his coffee.

"She's fine." He leaned down to stroke Smooch. "Yours?" he asked, indicating the orange cat.

"Yes. He's company for me. It gets lonely here at night...." She hadn't meant to say that, to say any-thing that sounded as though she was having trouble coping. "I like cats," she said. "Smooch is a lot of fun."

"Smooch? What is that?"

A smile quirked the corners of her lips. "It's an old-fashioned word for kissing and caressing. Well...petting. I mean Smooch is a pet and I..."

Armando nodded. "Yes, I understand." He put his coffee mug down. He stared at it for a moment, then said, "I lied before. I didn't have business in San Mig-uelito. I came because I wanted to see you, to make sure you were all right."

But that wasn't completely honest, either. He'd come because there hadn't been a moment since Susan had left that he hadn't thought about her. He kept remembering the way her face had looked in the moonlight, the way she moved, how soft her lips had been when he kissed her. He remembered his own unkindness.

"I was rude that night before you left," he said. "I'm sorry."

"No, it's all right." Susan's face flushed with embarrassment. "I understand. It must have been a shock—discovering I was pregnant, I mean."

He tightened his hand around the mug. "Yes, it was a shock." He looked at her and his dark eyes were serious. "I know it's not any of my business, Susana, but I'd like to know about it, about the baby's father I mean. Was it...is it a man you'd been going with for a long time? Someone you were in love with, someone you planned to marry?"

"No." Susan shook her head. "No, it wasn't like that."

"Tell me," Armando said.

She looked at him, then quickly away. She hadn't told anyone, not even Maria, exactly what had happened that night after the company party. She wasn't sure now that she wanted to talk about it, especially to Armando. She barely knew him; it would embarrass both of them.

"Please," he said. "I'd like to know."

She bent her head so that she wouldn't have to look at him. "He was a family friend," she said, "an older man, someone I'd known since I was a child."

Armando curled his hands around the coffee mug and waited.

"When I finished college and went to Houston, he helped me get a job in his law firm. We went out a few times."

She raised her face and he saw the distress in her amber eyes. He wanted to tell her to stop, but he couldn't. It was important for him to know about the other man because when he did, perhaps he could stop thinking about her.

"I never really thought of him as a date. He was someone to go out with, someone I felt safe and comfortable with." She hesitated. "We went to a company party. Zachary—that's his name, Zachary Owens—had too much to drink. When he took me home he asked if he could come in for a cup of coffee."

Her voice was so low that Armando had to strain to hear. He saw the rise and fall of her breasts and he wanted to say, Don't tell me. I don't want to hear any more. But he didn't speak. He looked at her bowed head and waited.

"I said that he could. We went in and he...before I could turn the light on he kissed me. I tried to push him away but I couldn't. He shoved me down on the sofa and then he was on top of me and he...he tore my dress. He ripped it all the way down and then he started pulling at the rest of my clothes and his clothes and—"

Armando came out of his chair. He knelt beside her and grasped her hands. "I'm sorry," he said in a voice choked with emotion. "You don't have to do this."

Tears were running down Susan's face, but she couldn't stop. "I tried to get away from him. I hit him and he...he grabbed my wrists and held them above my head and he said, 'You want it. You've been asking for it. Now you're going to get it.' And then he..." She couldn't go on.

"He raped you," Armando said.

Susan took a shuddering breath. "Yes," she whispered. "He raped me."

"*¡Madre de Dios!*" Armando tightened his grip on her hands. "Did you go to the police?"

She shook her head. "I was too ashamed. I thought it had been my fault, that maybe I'd led him on. That maybe, in some way, I was responsible."

"Of course you weren't responsible." He clenched his teeth so hard his jaw hurt. In a low and dangerous voice he said, "When something like this happens in Mexico we do not think it's a matter for the police. It is a family matter and the family takes care of it—of the man. When they are finished with him, he is never able to bother a woman again."

But Susana had no family, no one to look after her or see to the man's punishment. Armando wanted to gather her in his arms, to hold her and never let anything or anybody hurt her again. He understood her fear that night he had held her so close. She'd been afraid that he would force her, as the other man had forced her.

"What did you do when you saw him again?" he asked. "You worked at the same place. You would have had to see him."

"I quit my job. I didn't go back to the office. He called but I wouldn't speak to him, and when he came to the apartment I wouldn't let him in. I didn't see him until I knew I—I was pregnant. Then I went to his office because I thought he should know."

Armando's face was almost as white as hers now. "What did he say when you told him?"

"He was angry. He said I should have been on the pill. I told him there'd been no reason to be. I hadn't been...there hadn't been anyone..." She swallowed her shame. "He gave me a check for five thousand dollars, for an abortion, he said. I tore it up and threw it at him."

"You didn't consider an abortion?"

"No." Susan shook her head. "That was never a consideration. It's my baby."

"And his."

"No! It's not his. It's mine."

"You're going to keep it?"

"Yes, of course I'm going to keep it."

So many thoughts racketed around in his head, barging into each other, banging, fighting, beating in drumlike rhythm against his skull. Susana had been raped! A man had forced her, taken her against her will. And still she wanted to keep the baby. Why? In God's name why would she want to keep it? Women in her country believed in abortion, especially under circumstances like hers. She was alone. Her mother and father were dead. How could she raise a child alone?

"Why did you decide to come to Mexico?" he asked.

"It's where Maria was. She's my best friend, a friend from college."

"But when you knew she wouldn't be here, why did you come?"

"I don't know." A frown puckered Susan's forehead. "I didn't have anywhere else to go."

"Do you have any money?"

She nodded. "Money isn't a problem. Or at least it won't be for a year or so. I have the house where my parents lived and money my father left me. I'll be all right." She disentangled her hands from his. "Look," she said. "I shouldn't have dumped all of this on you. I'm sorry. I—"

"No, don't be sorry. I'm glad you told me." Armando stood up and shoved his hands into the pockets of his jeans. "I behaved very badly the night before you left the ranch, Susana. I'm sorry."

"No, Armando, I understand. I wasn't who or what you thought I was. That must have been a shock, especially here in Mexico where the customs are different."

Susan got up and went to stand beside him. "It's not that different in the United States. I'm sure any man I dated would feel the way you do. No man would want to...to see a woman who was carrying another man's child."

"I'm not every man," he said.

She looked up at him, questioning, full lower lip caught between small white teeth.

"I want to see you," he said. "I want to be your friend." He reached for her hand. "Now why don't you change and we'll go out for *comida*. I know a place on the other side of town that has the best *carne asada* in Mexico." And when Susan hesitated, he said, "Please, Susana. I want to be your friend."

Her friend. That made it clear what their relationship would be. And it was all right, Susan told herself. She would value Armando's friendship, and she would be careful never to cross the line between that and whatever emotion she had felt when Armando kissed her.

She held her hand out to him. "Friends," she said.

The *carne asada* was as good as Armando had said it would be. Susan ate every bite, along with the rice and beans and guacamole.

But she refused either a margarita or a glass of wine, saying, "No alcohol for me. Not until after the baby is born."

She'd felt guilty when she'd had a sip of wine with Armando at the ranch, and she'd spoken to Dr. Garcia at the clinic about drinking alcohol during her pregnancy.

"Before I knew I was pregnant I'd have a glass of wine occasionally," she'd said. "But that's about the extent of my drinking."

"I'd be happier if you didn't drink anything," Dr. Garcia had said.

And she had vowed not to.

"There's going to be a chamber-music concert Wednesday night," Armando said when he took Susan to her door that evening. "I'm sure you'd enjoy it. Why don't we have an early dinner first? I'll come at six. Is that all right?"

Susan nodded. "Yes, thank you, Armando, and thank you for the *comida*. It was delicious."

"Well then..." He brought her hand to his lips. "Good night, Susana."

"Good night, Armando."

But he stood there, still holding her hand. "Take care of yourself," he said.

"I will."

He wanted to cup her face between his hands and press his mouth to hers. He wanted to feel her body tremble against his, wanted to feel her soft and yielding against him. But he had promised himself when he came today that he would be her friend. Anything else was impossible.

And yet...

Moonlight shimmered over her shoulders and turned her skin to gold. If he didn't go quickly...

He dropped her hand. "Good night, Susana," he said. "Sleep well."

"You, too." She longed to take his hand again, to linger with him here in the moonlight. But she mustn't spoil the fragile relationship, the friendship that he offered.

"Good night," she said. "Drive safely."

"I will." He looked at her once more then, before he changed his mind, he turned and hurried across the patio.

He came back at noon the next day carrying a huge basket filled with mangoes and tangerines, oranges and apples and small green limes. On his second trip back from the pickup he brought a box of food that Juanita had prepared; a whole roasted chicken, a casserole of honeyed sweet potatoes, green beans, asparagus and fresh corn tortillas.

And a bouquet of red roses.

"Juanita was afraid you weren't eating properly," he told Susan. "She misses cooking for you. She wanted to be sure you had something for dinner."

Susan didn't know what to say. She was embarrassed, pleased that he had come, touched by his gift of food and the roses.

She managed to stammer her thanks as she led the way into the kitchen. And somewhere in the conversation she asked him to stay for dinner.

Armando helped her set the table out in the patio. He'd never done anything like that before, and it seemed strange to him to arrange the plates and the knives and forks on the dark blue tablecloth. Juanita would have been thunderstruck and Tia Inocencia would have hooted with laughter and called him a *mandilón*, a browbeaten man whose wife makes him help in the kitchen. But he enjoyed helping Susana.

Susan didn't have a stereo, so he found a radio station that played classical music and put that on while she poured wine for him and club soda with lime for herself.

When she placed the red roses in the middle of the table, she said, "The flowers are lovely, Armando. Thank you."

"You're welcome."

She looked young and adorably feminine in white shorts and a red cotton knit shirt that snugged tight over her breasts. He wondered if her breasts had grown larger with her pregnancy, and when she turned to the side to put a dish on the table he glanced quickly at her stomach. There wasn't any bulge. She looked fit and trim. If she hadn't told him, he wouldn't have known she was pregnant. But in another month or two... He bit the inside of his cheek. He didn't know how he would feel about her then.

"I forgot to tell you that I ran into Father Ramiro last week," Susan said when they sat down to eat. "He said to tell you to stop by and say hello to him."

"There's a Mass at six." Armando looked at his watch. "I could go to that and say hello to him afterward." He hesitated. "Would you like to come with me? I don't know whether or not you're Catholic—"

"No, I'm not."

"But you should see the church. It was built by the Franciscans in the late eighteen hundreds. It's really quite beautiful, Susana. We could have coffee with Father Ramiro after mass."

"All right," Susan said.

And after they had eaten and Armando had helped her with the dishes, she changed into a dress and went down the hill with him to the church on the plaza.

The Church of San Juan de Dios was beautiful in its simplicity. Sparkling chandeliers hung from the domed ceiling and over the altar. Rough stone arches opened off the main sanctuary into the smaller chapels. Angels and cherubs were carved into the retable above the candlelit altar. Christ on the cross looked from one side of the altar, Mary, His mother, from the other. A lace cloth covered the communion table.

Armando knelt when they entered their pew; Susan knelt beside him.

A bell from the tower rang the hour of evening Mass. A choir in the loft at the back of the church began to sing. And the Mass began.

Susan understood only a few words of the Spanish, but she liked being here. She'd felt very much a stranger these last two weeks, but sitting beside Armando, listening to a priest she knew and liked give the homily gave her a sense of belonging. She was glad that she had come.

They had coffee with Father Ramiro afterward and it was pleasant to sit with the two men, to listen to their friendly banter, to be a part of it.

When they left the restaurant, she and Armando walked the priest back to his home next to the church. And when they left him, Armando said, "We'd better get a taxi."

But Susan shook her head. "It's a lovely night. I'd like to walk."

"Up the hill?" He raised an eyebrow. "Isn't that difficult for you?"

She knew that he meant because of her pregnancy, but she said, "It was at first, but I've gotten used to both the altitude and the climb."

The night was quiet. There was no one in the central plaza, and as they made their way up the cobblestone streets they saw only one or two people. When they started the steep climb up to her house, Armando took her hand.

"Be careful," he cautioned. "You could fall if you stepped on a loose stone." He thought about her coming up and down the street alone. "Don't do this alone at night," he said. "And be careful when you're walking down during the day."

"Muy bien," she said with a smile.

"You're speaking Spanish." He seemed surprised.

"I've enrolled in a class. I go every day from nine until one. I'm still not very good, but it's coming along."

"Good for you." Armando put his arm around her waist and as quickly pulled away.

When they reached her gate they went in and he took Susan to the door.

"Thank you," she said. "For the food and the flowers, and for taking me to church with you."

"You're welcome." Armando hesitated, strangely reluctant to leave her. "I'll see you Wednesday at six," he said.

Susan nodded. "Good night, Armando. It's been a lovely day."

"Yes, it has." He wanted, more than he'd ever wanted anything in his life, to kiss her. And because he knew that he couldn't, he brought her hand to his lips.

His lips were cool against her skin. She wanted to touch the top of his head. To bury her fingers in his thick curly hair. To hold him here, keep him here.

"Good night," she said again.

Armando let go of her hand. "Good night, Susana."

If he stayed a moment longer he would take her in his arms. He would kiss her until they were both weak with longing. He would...

He stepped away from her. "Until Wednesday," he said.

Then he was gone, striding through the patio and out of the gate. She heard the pickup start and watched until he drove away.

Chapter Five

The dream came again that night and with it, a fear so dark and cold that she was unable to move. Her breathing grew labored, her skin hurt from holding herself so tightly.

She screamed, mouth open, throat working, but no sound came. She tried to run, but her legs were slow and heavy.

He crept toward her through the darkness. She tried again to cry out and the sound came, weak and ineffective. The heaviness of his body crushed down upon her, holding her captive.

Had to break free. Had to escape. Body not cold now but covered with the sweat of fear.

"No, no, no, no...!"

Susan's eyes opened. She sat straight up in bed, terrified and gasping for breath. "No!" she said again into the silence of the room. Maria's room. Dying embers smoldered in the fireplace. Smooch meowed and blinked his yellow eyes, annoyed at being awakened.

Still trembling, needing the warmth of a living thing next to her, Susan pulled the kitten into her arms. The dream had come many times since the night Zachary had . . . Since the night of the company party. She shivered with the memory and willed herself to calmness.

At last, soothed by the gentle purring of the kitten, she closed her eyes and slept.

The weather turned cold on Tuesday. By Wednesday morning the temperature was in the low fifties and a crisp wind blew down from the mountains. On her way back from her class Susan stopped in the market and bought a heavy blue wool poncho to wear when she went out with Armando.

That night she put on a pale blue dress and, for the first time since she'd been in San Miguelito, a pair of high heels. Armando would be driving tonight; she wouldn't have to walk on cobblestones.

He brought her a bouquet of lavender roses when he came, and when she was putting them in water he said, "I like your dress. You look very pretty tonight, Susana." And because he wanted to touch her, he turned away and went to one of the windows overlooking the town and stayed there with his back to her until she said, "I'm ready, Armando."

The restaurant that he chose for dinner was on the lake, just outside of San Miguelito.

"It's cold tonight," he said when the waiter led them to a table near the huge stone fireplace. "Do you have any heat in the house?"

"Just the fireplaces in the living room and bedroom. But it's enough."

"It may not be later on. You'd better think about getting some kind of a heater." He took the poncho off her shoulders and folded it in an empty chair.

"It gets colder than this?"

Armando nodded. "We're almost seven thousand feet above sea level, Susana. It rarely freezes, but it can get down into the thirties at night."

"And all this time I thought I was in sunny Mexico."

"You are and it is, sunny, I mean. During the day it'll be warm, it's just the mornings and nights when you'll need the heat." He looked at her curiously. "I know you're busy with school during the day, but what about at night. What do you do?"

"I study my lesson for the next day." She shrugged. "I don't know, Armando. I read. Sometimes I bake cookies or fix something for dinner the next day."

"I have an extra television at the ranch. I'll bring it next time I come."

"No, really, I don't mind not having TV. I brought some tapes with me and I listen to music or to the radio. I'm even beginning to understand some of it, *poco a poco*." She looked at him. "Little by little? Is that right?"

Armando nodded. "It's perfect." He smiled as the waiter approached their table, and after he had ordered for both of them, said, "I don't like the thought of your being there alone at night, Susana. You don't know anyone, you don't have any close neighbors. Couldn't you arrange for Esperanza to stay with you?"

"I wouldn't want to." She buttered a hot *bolillo*. "Besides, Esperanza has a family, six boys and four girls. She has to be home with them at night."

"I wish you'd consider moving in with Aunt Inocencia and her mother. I've spoken to them about you—"

"About my being pregnant?" she asked sharply.

"No, of course not. I only said that you were young and alone and that your house was more than a mile from town. I said I wished you were living with a family, someone who could look after you."

"I'm twenty-three years old. I'm quite capable of taking care of myself."

"But you're *embarazada*, pregnant. What if you should fall?"

"I'll pick myself up." It was kind of Armando to be concerned, but she didn't like him fussing over her like this.

"I've invited Inocencia and Sophia for dinner next Sunday," he said. "You'll enjoy meeting them."

"Armando, I..." Susan shook her head. "I'm not sure I should do that, meet your family, I mean." She waited while the waiter served their salad and when he had gone she said, "Maybe we shouldn't see so much of each other, Armando."

His dark eyebrows came together in a frown. "Why not?"

"Because of my...my situation. You're a handsome young man—"

"I'm thirty-two."

"All right, thirty-two. I'm sure you know a lot of attractive single women who don't have my kind of a problem." She picked up her glass of club soda. "In another month or so I'll begin to show. I don't want to embarrass you or your family." She put the glass of club soda down without having tasted it. "I know how you feel about my pregnancy. I saw it on your face the night I told you."

"I was surprised. I said things I didn't mean."

"I understand why you did, and I know you're being nice to me now because I don't know anybody. I appreciate it, Armando, and I love being with you. But I'm okay. I'm healthy and happy and I'm going to have a healthy, happy baby. So don't worry about me. I'm—"

She stopped again as the waiter served their food, broiled white fish for her and a steak for Armando. They ate in silence for a few minutes, then he said, "I enjoy being with you, Susana."

More than he'd ever enjoyed being with a woman before. There was something about her, a warmth, an inner glow that made her almost ethereally beautiful. In the softness of candlelight her amber eyes were golden, her pale skin like ivory touched with the color of summer roses.

Soon her belly would grow large with another man's child. How would he feel then? he wondered. Would he want to stop seeing her? And if he did, wouldn't it be better to stop now? He didn't want to hurt her. Perhaps she was right. Perhaps they should stop.... He looked at her across the table. "I'll pick you up at two o'clock on Sunday," he said.

The concert was held in an old, refurbished granary. It was a long, narrow building, with lights hanging from the high ceiling and spotlights illuminating the stage. Straight-backed chairs had been arranged to seat three hundred people.

Armando nodded to a few acquaintances, then led Susan to their seats near the front. The place filled quickly with well-dressed men and women from both the Mexican and the American communities. A man with photographic equipment sat at one side against the wall.

"Tonight they're playing Prokofiev and Beethoven," Armando said when he handed Susan a program. "I hope you'll enjoy it."

"I know I will." She liked the atmosphere here, the stark white stucco walls with the simple but classic wool wall hangings in warm earth tones, the unadorned stage, empty except for the baby grand piano that had been polished to a high sheen.

At eight o'clock the audience quieted. The musicians, a pianist and a violinist, came down the center aisle. The pianist sat at the piano and a man came up on the stage and stood next to it so that he could turn the music pages.

The two musicians nodded. All but two stage lights were turned off. The concert began.

Susan closed her eyes and let herself drift with the music. It surrounded and enfolded her, and soon everything else was forgotten in the beauty of the Prokofiev sonata.

Minutes passed. Then suddenly, without warning, the lights over the stage went out and the granary plunged into total darkness. The musicians didn't hesitate, they continued playing, and the music soared, gloriously, majestically, there in the total darkness of the old building.

A man ran up the aisle with a flashlight, with which he illuminated the pianist's music. The photographer directed his camera light toward the violinist.

A surrealistic magic held the audience spellbound, joined in this small space of time in perfect communion with the creator of the music and the musicians who played it.

Armando reached for Susan's hand and closed his fingers around hers. For a little while she listened with her eyes closed, and when she opened them she barely managed to smother a gasp. On the white wall behind the stage the shadow of the violinist, giant sized in silhouette, cradled his violin in an attitude part pain, part passion, his bow a magic wand as the timeless music rose heavenward.

Her eyes luminous with the sheer beauty of the music and the moment, Susan turned to look at Armando. She saw his lips part and heard the whisper of her name, "Susana." And when he put his arm around her and drew her close, she didn't move away. She leaned her head against his shoulder and together, there in the darkness, they listened to the music that must surely have been made in heaven.

Armando kept his arm around her when they left the concert and walked down the road to where he had parked his car. He opened the door and helped her in, then got in on the other side. He looked at her for a moment, then without a word he drew her into his arms.

"Susana," he said. "Susana."

Her lips parted and softened. He kissed her gently, his mouth undemanding, tender. And when the kiss ended he rested his face against hers.

They stayed like that for a long moment. He kissed her throat, and then her lips again, briefly this time before he turned to start the car. But he didn't let her go, he kept one arm around her, and when she rested her head against his shoulder, he sighed with a contentment more profound than any he'd ever known.

When he stopped outside her gate, he took her hand and said, "I'll come in with you so that I can build up the fire in both fireplaces. Whenever you want me to leave, I will."

A quiver of nerves, and something more, ran through Susan. She hesitated only a fraction of a second before she nodded and said, "Thank you, Armando," and handed him her key.

It was cold inside. With a shiver Susan pulled the poncho closer and said, "I'll make some hot chocolate while you light the fires."

Armando went into her bedroom and after he had switched on the light on the table beside her bed, he knelt in front of the fireplace and began laying wood, pieces of twigs and newspaper. The orange kitten padded in, looked him over, meowed, then tail aloft, sailed out of the room.

When the fire caught and held, Armando went into the living room and did the same with the fireplace there. By the time Susan came in with the hot chocolate, the fire was blazing and the room had begun to warm. The kitten lay curled up on the hearth.

They sat together on the sofa facing the fireplace. "I love a fire," Susan said. "We didn't have one in our house in Granbury, but I had an aunt who had a place on the beach in Galveston. She liked fireplaces as much as I did, and whenever she knew I was coming to visit she laid a fire. That warming fire was always the first thing I saw."

"That's nice. You must have loved her very much."

"Yes, I did."

He put the mug of hot chocolate down on the coffee table. "Something happened between us tonight, Susana."

Susana looked at him. "Yes, I know."

He took the mug of chocolate out of her hand and put it on the table beside his. Then, with his arm around her shoulders, he leaned back against the sofa. For a long time they didn't speak, they only watched the orange flames.

It had been a very long time since Susan had felt this comforting sense of warmth that comes only when there is a bonding between people who care for each other. She didn't ever want to move, she wanted to stay within the circle of Armando's arms.

With a finger under her chin he raised her face. For a moment he only looked at her. Her lips parted. She whispered his name and her eyes drifted closed.

His lips were warm and undemanding at first, but little by little the kiss changed. He tightened his arms around her and said, "My sweet Susana." And when she touched his face and whispered, "Armando, oh, Armando," he slipped the blue poncho from her shoulders and drew her close into his embrace. He knew he should stop now. If he didn't stop soon...

Susan's hands crept up around his neck. Her delicate fingers threaded through his hair. Her mouth was hot and moist.

"We should stop," she whispered.

"I know." He brought her closer. "I know," he murmured against the scented cloud of her hair.

Her breasts pushed softly against his chest. He had to touch her. Had to... He cupped her breast and her hand came up to stay him. "Only for a moment," he said, and she withdrew her hand.

She was so soft. Her breast fit so snugly in his hand. He caressed her through her blue wool dress and ran his fingers over the rigid peaks that pressed against the fabric.

It wasn't enough. He reached for the back zipper of her dress and eased it down. Susan stilled but didn't move.

Something was happening to her body that had never happened before. It was as though every nerve ending had been touched with electricity. Her lips were warm with life, seeking, tasting, eager for his lips. And when he pushed her bra aside and touched her naked breasts, her body quivered with pleasure.

Almost beside herself with the need to touch him, Susan began to fumble with the buttons of his shirt.

"Wait," Armando whispered. He let her go and took his tweed jacket off and tossed it aside, then opened his shirt. When she made as though to move toward him he put one arm around her and brought her down to lie beside him on the sofa. It was glorious to feel her next to him, her breasts against his bare chest, the long lovely legs so close to his.

Then, unbidden, he thought, I wonder if this is the first time she has made love since she was raped? And he thought of how it might have been for her to have been taken against her will.

"Susana," he whispered against her mouth. He brought her closer, and he wanted, more than he'd ever wanted anything before, to ease the hurt that had been inflicted on her, to make the memory disappear.

His curly chest hair tickled and teased her breasts. She rubbed them back and forth against him, too excited now for caution, reveling in the thrill of sensations that coursed through her body.

He sought her lips. He said, "Do you know what you're doing to me? Do you?" He kissed her again and his hands found her breasts. He cupped their sweet fullness and leaned to kiss them, first one then the other.

Susan tightened her hands on his shoulders. It was too much, past bearing, he had to stop.

He slid his hands under her back, holding her closer, a captive of his hungry mouth.

A captive. A shock of fear ran through her body. The flash of a dream streaked dark and ugly across her brain. She whispered, "No," but Armando didn't hear. He flicked his tongue across her nipple. She tried to move away. He flicked again. This time she shivered with pleasure and the dream was forgotten.

The skirt of the blue dress hiked up around her hips. Armando felt her silk-clad thighs against his own. He'd never wanted a woman as much as he wanted Susana.

He let her go and sat up. In a voice shaking with need he said, "Susana, we have to stop. I can't control the way I feel. If I don't stop now..."

She reached up and brushed a lock of hair back off his forehead. Then she wet her lips and said, "I—I don't want you to stop."

Armando stared down at her and an emotion unlike anything he'd ever known before clogged his throat. She was so beautiful; her eyes, her tender mouth, her lovely breasts. He kissed her, then he helped her to sit up and then to stand. Without a word he drew her over in front of the fire. He slipped the blue dress down over her hips and when she stepped out of it, he tossed it onto a chair. She stood there, watching him, clad only in silk stockings, a narrow blue garter belt and blue bikini panties, arms at her sides, waiting.

"Now you," Susan whispered. And she watched, as though hypnotized, while Armando undid his belt and drew it through the tabs that held it. Watched as he eased the zipper down, pulled the pants low over his hips and stepped out of them. Watched when he hooked his thumbs under the sides of his low-riding briefs.

He stood naked before her, his skin bronzed by the fire, muscled and magnificent. His shoulders were broad, his waist and hips narrow, his legs as beautifully sculptured as Michelangelo's *David*.

"Come here," he said hoarsely.

Susan took a tentative step toward him.

He put his hands on her shoulders and drew her close. "Susana," he said, and gently kissed her. Then he picked her up in his arms and carried her into the bedroom.

She shivered when he set her down, whether from sudden nerves or from the cold, he wasn't sure. It hadn't yet heated up in here as it had in the living room, except in front of the fire, so with a smile Armando pulled the down comforter off the bed and brought it back to the fireplace. He laid it over the braided rug in front of the fire, and knelt down to smooth it out. Then he raised his hand to her, and when Susan knelt beside him he clasped her in his arms and kissed her with all of the passion he'd been holding in check until this moment. And when she lay down, he slid the satin panties and the garter belt and the silk stockings down over her hips.

He couldn't wait. With a low cry he covered her body with his. He wanted her now with an urgency he could no longer control. He grasped her hips and pushed her legs apart with his knee...

The way Zachary had.

Terror came, black and cold and unbidden. With a strangled cry Susan pushed him away from her. "No, don't!" she cried. "Let me go! Let me go!"

Armando drew back. "What is it?" he said. "Susana, what is it?"

"Don't touch me! Don't . . ." She stared up at him, then with a low cry of anguish she rolled onto her stomach and began to weep.

"I don't understand. What's the matter? What . . . ?" Then he knew. She had been raped, taken against her will. He stared helplessly down at her, wanting to kill the man who had done this to her. His hands closed into fists, as he imagined them closing on her attacker's throat. But the man, whoever he was, didn't matter now. He had to think of Susana.

He touched her shoulder. "Don't cry," he said. "We won't do anything you don't want to do."

She didn't answer, nor did she try to move away. She was so ashamed, so sorry. She had led him on. She'd let him undress her and bring her in here. Then, like a crazy person, she'd shoved him away.

"It's all right," he said. "I understand, Susana." He stroked her back, soothing her, calming her. And when at last she turned to face him he said again, "I understand."

"I'm sorry," she whispered. "I'm so sorry, Armando."

He smoothed the tumbled hair away from her face. "There's no need to be."

She struggled to speak more calmly. "You must think I'm crazy. That I'm a tease . . ." She turned her head so that he wouldn't see the shame in her eyes.

Armando touched the side of her face. "I don't think anything, Susana," he said. "I told you that I understand, and I do." And when she shivered, from cold as well as from reaction, he helped her to sit up and said, "We'd better get you into bed."

She stood up, and when she tried to hide her nakedness, Armando picked the comforter up and put it around her before he led her to the bed. He turned back the heavy blankets, then took the comforter from her and when she lay down, he put it over the blankets.

"It's so cold," she said, and hugged her arms across her chest.

He stood for a moment, looking down at her. Then he lifted the blankets and came into the bed beside her.

"What are you...?" Her eyes widened with fear. "No, don't. You said you wouldn't...." She tried to back away from him.

But Armando drew her into his arms. "I just want to hold you, to warm you." He put his hand against the back of her head and pressed her face to his shoulder. "Nothing is going to harm you, Susana. Go to sleep now. I'll be here."

"No, please—"

"Shh," he said and kissed the top of her head. "Go to sleep, *querida*."

Her body was stiff and unyielding, but as he held her and whispered to her, half in English, half in Spanish, she relaxed. Soon she grew warm and her eyes grew heavy.

"Sleep," he said. "Sleep, Susana."

At last, safe and warm in the comfort of Armando's arms, she closed her eyes.

And that night, for the first time in a long time, the dream did not come.

Chapter Six

Armando awoke as the first streaks of dawn lighted the sky. He lay for a moment, disoriented, until he became aware of Susan. She lay with her head against his shoulder, one arm around his waist, the spill of her marvelous chestnut hair splayed across his chest. He remembered then how it had been last night, her earlier passion, and her fear.

He thought of all the other women he had known and wondered if he would have exercised such restraint with any of them. He did not think he would have, but there had been something about this young American woman that touched him, that made him want to take care of her.

He had slept with her last night. He had held her without passion...no, that wasn't quite true. He had wanted her as he'd never wanted a woman before but he had been able to sublimate his desires to Susana's needs.

Her fear and her vulnerability had touched him. He'd wanted to protect her, even from himself.

It had been a long time before he had been able to sleep because he'd been so painfully aware of the softness of her breath against his skin, of her womanly curves and the press of her breasts against his chest.

He knew he should get up now, before she awakened. He didn't know what time her maid came, but he thought it would embarrass Susan to have her maid find him here.

Susan murmured in her sleep and he put his arms around her to bring her closer. Without waking, she nuzzled against him, soft and warm and so infinitely desirable that it took every bit of his willpower not to touch her.

Armando thought then of the man who had raped Susan, and without conscious thought his arms tightened protectively around her. He'd never before realized what it must be like for a woman to be taken against her will, of what it must do to her, emotionally, psychologically.

There were men who made jokes about rape. He remembered overhearing one of his classmates at the university in Texas saying, "Hell, man, they all want it. Maybe some of them pretend they don't, but they do. The way I see it, you buy a woman a decent dinner, you've got the right to expect a little action. It's like the old joke, if rape is inevitable, they should relax and enjoy it."

Because of the man, the family friend, who had raped her, Susan was afraid of the act of love. Last night he had wondered if he was the first to have tried to make love to her since the rape, and knew now that he was.

How long, he wondered, would she live with the terror of remembrance?

His jaw clenched hard with the certainty of what he would do if he ever met the man who had done this to her. And he asked himself, as he had since the afternoon Susan had told him about the rape, why she would want to keep the child. She had been taken against her will by a man who had given no thought to her feelings. Abortion was against his Catholic beliefs, but Susana wasn't Catholic. Why, then, had she chosen to carry the child? Did she mean to have it and then to put it up for adoption? Surely she didn't intend to raise it.

Now, in the early morning light that streamed into the room, she looked so young that it was difficult for him to imagine there was a child growing inside her. She had natural, well-shaped dark eyebrows, a straight nose and a sweetly curved mouth. Her lower lip was full and ripe and infinitely kissable. If he leaned toward her he could take her mouth, he could...

Armando's body hardened with the need again. Hot and urgent, it surged through his body, tightening his loins, making him gasp with fresh desire. He knew that if he didn't leave her now he wouldn't leave at all. He tried to disengage his arms. Susan murmured in protest and moved closer. Her breasts pressed against his side, her thighs close to his hip.

Armando gritted his teeth. With a smothered moan, he pushed back the heavy blankets. But when he did, Susan buried her face against the side of his neck.

He tried to move away from her. "Go back to sleep," he said. "I'm going to build a fire so the room will be warm when you get up."

Her eyes opened slowly and focused on his face. "Armando? What are you...?" Her eyes widened.

Armando was in bed with her. Had they made love? Had he...? She remembered then. They'd *almost* made love, but she had stopped because she was afraid. Armando had put her to bed. He had slept with her. But he hadn't touched her, not in a sexual way. Even now, when she lay here in his arms, he held her as gently as he would a child.

Susan took a deep, tremulous breath. "You've been here all night," she said.

Armando nodded. "I couldn't leave you."

"I'm so sorry for the way I acted, Armando. I led you on. I let you kiss me..." She shook her head. "What a fool you must think me," she whispered.

"I don't think you're a fool, Susana. I think you've been badly hurt by what happened to you. I should have known that. I should have been more careful."

"It wasn't your fault, Armando. It was the concert, that wonderful music and the fireplace and..." She tried to smile. "Let's blame it on the hot chocolate. Okay? Let's just say that the hot chocolate went to our heads?" She smiled shyly, then her smile faded because she suddenly realized that she and Armando were practically nose to nose and that both of them were naked. A flush crept into her cheeks. "I—I guess I'd better get up now."

"It's barely light." His body throbbed with wanting her, but he was afraid to move. "Susana?" He touched the side of her face and when she didn't turn away, he ran his thumb across her lips.

"You're so beautiful," he said. Then, because he could not help himself, he kissed her. "You feel so good," he whispered against her lips.

Good? She set him on fire. Her mouth was warm and alive under his. When her lips softened he dared to slip his tongue past her parted lips, and when her tongue met his he gasped with pleasure. He went slowly. With infinite care he began to stroke her breasts. Like a cat she stretched and sighed and arched her back.

A flame came to life somewhere deep inside her. Each time he touched her, it grew brighter, hotter. She curled her fingers into his dark thatch of chest hair and moved them up to his shoulders. She loved the texture of his skin under her fingertips, and when he began to kiss her breasts, she nuzzled his neck and pressed soft wet kisses against his throat and his ears. And shivered with pleasure when he moaned softly against her breast.

He came up then to reclaim her mouth, and when he had kissed her he said, "Yes, Susana?" And his Spanish-green eyes were hooded with a passion that both frightened and excited her.

"Yes," she said so softly he could barely hear her.

Armando kissed her again. He covered her body with his, but for a moment he didn't move, he only waited. If she drew away, if she asked him to stop... But she didn't. She put her arms around him, and when he entered her she sighed and said, "Oh yes."

Her softness closed in around him, holding him, warming him. He moved against her, slowly, carefully, luxuriating in the silken feel of her.

Susan lifted her body to his. She followed where he led and murmured with pleasure, not with fear.

He said her name, "Susana, Susana," over and over again. He whispered words in Spanish she didn't understand, and all the while he moved deeper and faster within her.

She had not known it could be like this. The ecstasy grew until it was past bearing. Her arms were around him, holding him close as her body moved against his.

The flame became a fire she could no longer control. She met him thrust for thrust, wanting him, needing him.

Her breath came faster. She whispered, "Armando, oh, Armando," and thought her body would burst with pleasure. "Please," she whispered. "Oh, darling..."

He brought her even closer, and suddenly she was out of control, unable to hold back, climbing higher and higher to a place she'd never been before, clinging to him, one with him, sobbing his name in an ecstasy of release.

He took her mouth and her cry and mingled it with his own. *"Mi preciosa,"* he whispered. *"Mi querida* Susana."

His body quivered with reaction as he buried his face in the fullness of her hair and tightened his arms around her. He breathed in the scent of her, the warmth of her. He kissed her eyes, her nose and her cheeks. He told her how lovely she was and how she made him feel.

Susan clung to him, trembling in the aftermath of love. And when he whispered, "Go back to sleep," she snuggled against him.

When she was asleep, Armando got up and showered and dressed. When he came out of the bathroom, the orange kitten rubbed against his legs and he picked it up and went into the kitchen. He found a can of cat food in the cupboard and opened it while the kitten wove in between and around his legs.

"Paciencia," he said, and when he put the food down, the kitten pushed his head against Armando's hand and with a meow began to eat.

He made a cup of coffee for himself and took it into the living room where he stirred up the remains of last night's fire and added small pieces of wood and newspaper. After he got that fire started he went into the bedroom and, careful not to wake Susan, built a fire there. Then he went back into the kitchen again and made hot chocolate. When it was ready he carried it into the bedroom.

She opened one eye when she heard him. Then she smiled, and gathering the comforter around her, sat up in bed.

Armando sat beside her. He handed the mug to her, cautioning, "Be careful, it's hot."

She took a sip. "It's delicious," she said. "Thank you."

"I have to leave, Susana. I've got things to do at the ranch. I'll call you later, and I'll see you on Sunday." He kissed her. "You make me very happy," he said.

"And you make me feel whole again." She hesitated, trying to find the words to tell him. "I didn't know making love could be like that." She touched his face. "Thank you for this morning, Armando. And thank you for last night."

He took the hand that rested against his face and kissed her palm. He wanted to take her in his arms again, but he knew that if he did he wouldn't be able to let her go. So he said, "It's cold this morning. Dress warmly when you go out. I'll call you tonight."

When he had gone Susan leaned back against the pillows and closed her eyes. She had never known anyone like Armando Cobian. He had slept with her last night, cradled her and held her, and all of the fear, all of the bad dreams had gone away. She hadn't known, hadn't even suspected, that anything could be as thrillingly wonderful as what she had experienced in his arms this morning.

But how could what had begun between them continue? In another month or two her body would swell with the life inside. How would Armando feel about her then? Would he still want to make love to her? Would he even want to be seen with her?

Susan put down the mug of hot chocolate and knuckled away the tears. Wouldn't it be better to end this now so that neither of them would be hurt?

Armando would be an easy man to fall in love with. She had to end it before that happened. Before... Susan closed her eyes. It had already happened; she had fallen in love with Armando Cobian.

And she didn't know what to do about that.

"Tia Inocencia and Sophia came to the ranch right after church," Armando told Susan when he went to pick her up on Sunday. "They're anxious to meet you."

Susan smiled uncertainly, not at all sure how she felt about meeting his family.

Armando had arrived a little after eleven o'clock, earlier than she had expected him, with a bag of fresh pastry and a bouquet of daisies. He kissed her, then while she found a vase for the daisies, he prepared a pot of tea.

"We won't eat until four," he said. "You need to have something before we leave."

When the tea was ready and he'd found a plate for the pastry, he fixed a tray and placed it in front of the sofa. Then with a smile he said, "Come here," and gathered her in his arms.

"I've missed you. I've thought about you every moment I've been gone." He held her away so that he could look at her. "I wanted to come back last night and the night before, but I had business to attend to. Two men from Costa Rica were at the ranch. They bought twenty of my best horses. I took them to the train this morning.''

He cupped her face. "I've been telling myself ever since I left here that I had only imagined how beautiful you are. But I didn't imagine it, you really are the most beautiful creature I've ever seen." He brushed his lips against hers. "My darling Susana," he murmured. "Whatever did I do without you?"

"Armando—"

"I love the way you say my name." He brought her closer so that their lips were barely touching. "Say it again."

"Armando," she whispered against his lips.

"Yes," he sighed. And he took the word and her lips and kissed her with all the hunger that had been building for the days he'd been away from her.

He wanted her again, but because he sensed a reticence about her this morning, he picked up his cup of tea and settled back against the sofa. He had told her he'd come for her at two, so she hadn't been expecting him. Her face, without makeup, looked scrubbed and clean. She was dressed in jeans, a faded navy blue sweatshirt and fuzzy blue slippers. It seemed so natural, so homey, to be sitting here with her on a Sunday morning, sipping tea in front of a fire.

The thought startled him; it gave him pause. Whoa, he told himself. Take it easy, hombre. Susana's a lovely woman, but . . .

But what? Don't get involved? Because she's pregnant? He shoved the thought away. It wasn't her fault that she was pregnant. But if she'd had an abortion there wouldn't be a problem.

"Your tea's getting cold," Susan said. She bit into a piece of pastry and a powdered-sugar moustache coated her upper lip.

"Come here," Armando said, and before she could object he brought her close and began to lick her sugared lips. "Umm," he murmured. "You taste good." He kissed her then, and when he did he forgot that he'd told himself to take it easy. She was warm and soft in his arms, loving and loveable. He slid his hand under the navy-blue sweatshirt and reached up to touch her breasts.

A sigh escaped her lips. "We can't," she said. "We have to go. I have to dress."

"We have time." He eased her back against the sofa. "Are you wearing anything under your jeans?" he asked.

"Armando, we . . . we shouldn't."

"Are you?"

Susan shook her head. She wanted to tell him to stop because she had decided they shouldn't make love anymore. The other morning had happened. But it mustn't happen again.

He pushed the sweatshirt up and began to kiss her breasts.

"No, please," she whispered.

"Please what?" he asked. He flicked one peaked breast with his tongue. "Please this?" He took the nipple between his teeth and gently scraped. "Or this? Tell me, Susana. Tell me what you like?"

She clutched his shoulders. "We shouldn't," she said again.

"Why, sweetheart? Tell me why?"

But when she tried to speak he kissed her, hard and deep, and when he let her go, her body trembled with the same need she felt coursing through his.

He unfastened her jeans and pulled the zipper down. "You make me feel like a teenager," he said. "I look at you and I forget all propriety. All I can think of is how much I want you." He slid the jeans over her hips and down her ankles.

For a moment he only looked at her, lying there naked before him. Then he undressed and tossed his clothes aside. "Susana," he said, then he came down beside her.

Susan put her arms around him. "I can't help it," she said, more to herself than to him. "I know we shouldn't, but I can't—"

He kissed away her words and with a cry, no longer able to wait, he joined his body to hers. They moved quickly, without restraint, clinging and close. Just before that final moment he kissed her and felt the tears upon her face.

"What is it?" he asked. But then the moment came, for her and for him. His body spun out of control and everything else but the unbelievable pleasure of the moment was forgotten.

It was only later, on the way to the ranch, that Armando remembered her tears.

At ninety, Sophia Rodriquez was a thin, birdlike old lady with snow-white hair and an autocratic bearing. She peered at Susan through glasses that seemed too heavy for her face, raised her voice and asked in Spanish, "Why aren't you having any sherry?"

"I—I don't drink."

"*De veras*, really? I thought all *Norteamericanos* drank."

"Not all, Mother. Not any more than all Mexicans drink." Inocencia smiled at Susan. "Mama has many preconceived ideas," she said in English.

"*¿Como?* Speak up girl." Sophia cupped a hand over her ear. "What did you say?"

"I said not all Americans drink."

Sophia frowned and thumped her cane on the tile floor. "I have heard it on good authority that they do." She turned her attention back to Susan. "How do you come to know Armando?"

Susan looked at him. "I'm sorry," she said. "I don't understand.

A smile quirked the corners of his mouth. "Aunt Sophia is being curious. She wants to know how we met." He said something to the elderly woman, and she answered, *"Ah, muy bien,"* and finally offered Susan a smile.

"What did you tell her?" she asked Armando.

"That we met in church when Father Ramiro introduced us."

Now it was Susan's turn to smile. "Shame on you," she said, forgetting for a moment that Inocencia spoke English. "Father Ramiro did introduce us," she told the younger woman. "But it was on the train from Nuevo Laredo."

"But Armando has made my mother happy," Inocencia said with a laugh. "You see, she's nodded off, quite content now that she knows that the two of you met in a proper manner."

Not quite proper, Susan thought, and decided not to explain to Inocencia she'd been stranded and that Armando had brought her here to his ranch for a week.

At sixty-two Inocencia Rodriquez was still an attractive woman. She was tall, and though she was not heavy, she had ample breasts, a surprisingly narrow waist and flaring hips. She wore her auburn hair in a chignon, and though she had pulled it back, soft tendrils of it had escaped to curl around her face in a most becoming manner.

Susan wondered about Inocencia's friend Francisco, the man who had waited all these years to marry her. What kind of a man was he? When would his patience grow thin? From the looks of Inocencia's mother, Sophia would last at least another ten years. And then, of course, there would be Inocencia's brothers to contend with.

And because she hated the thought of this attractive woman spending her life without the man she loved, Susan said, "I'm so sorry you didn't bring your friend Francisco with you today. I was going to invite Armando to dinner on Thursday. I'd love to have you and Francisco join us."

"Susana, really." Armando frowned. "I doubt that Francisco would be available. Besides, Inocencia goes to her woman's meeting on Thursday nights. She's been going for years, haven't you, Inocencia?"

"Yes, for years." Inocencia looked from one to the other of them. "But I appreciate your invitation, Señorita Susana."

"Then shall we make it Friday?" Susan persisted.

"Friday?" Inocencia wet her lips. Her ample bosom rose as she took a deep breath. She looked at Armando, then at her sleeping mother. "I'll speak to Francisco," she said. "But yes, I'm—I'm sure Friday will be fine."

"Wonderful! Shall we say at seven? Armando can explain where I live." Then, because she knew he was furious with her, Susan began to talk about the house she'd taken over from Maria and how much she loved San Miguelito. "The view is beautiful," she said. "I can see all of the town, the lake and the distant mountains. The sunsets are incredible."

"But aren't you lonely, living alone I mean? Do you have any neighbors close by?"

"Not really. But I walk into town every day. I'm taking Spanish classes, and I've met a few people in the class." Susan smiled. "I hope one of these days my Spanish will be as good as your English."

"Thank you. I rarely have the opportunity to use it."

"Does Francisco speak English?"

Inocencia nodded. "He's an attorney. Many of his clients are North Americans."

"I look forward to meeting him." Only then did Susan took a chance and look at Armando. Though his face was composed she knew he was furious.

When Juanita announced that the *comida* was ready, Susan linked her arm through Inocencia's and let Armando escort Sophia into the dining room where the candlelit table welcomed them.

The meal began with a clear consommé. That was followed by a salad, white fish, rice with dried shrimp and a rack of lamb.

Sophia ate everything Juanita placed before her. She had an extra helping of lamb, and when the dessert of mango pie topped with ice cream came, she had two helpings.

"Mama has a fine appetite," Inocencia said.

Which seemed to Susan to be the understatement of the year.

When coffee had been served, with a brandy for both Armando and Sophia, Sophia began to question Susan, using Armando as an interpreter.

She wanted to know Susan's age, where her parents were and why they had permitted her to travel to Mexico alone.

"Susan's parents are dead," Armando told her.

"Ay, pobrecita." Sophia patted Susan's hand. *"Estás sola. Que triste. ¿Pero, por qué estás en Mexico?"*

"She said it's very sad that you're alone," Armando translated. And not quite meeting Susan's eyes added, "She's curious about why you came to Mexico?"

"Tell her I was saddened by my father's recent death, and, because I've always wanted to come to Mexico, I thought a change of scene would help my sadness."

"Yes, that's best for now," he said in English before he turned to speak to Sophia.

For now? What about later when her pregnancy began to show? he wondered. What would he tell Sophia and Inocencia then?

He had wanted them to meet Susan because they were a part of his family. Sophia had always treated him as a son, Inocencia, as a younger brother. He could see that both of them liked Susan, but how would they feel when they learned that she was pregnant? And unmarried?

There'd be an uproar and a scandal. Everybody in the family, every distant cousin and every in-law, scattered all over Mexico from Sonora to Jalisco, would know that he was seeing a woman made pregnant by another man.

But he wouldn't think about that now.

At eight o'clock Sophia yawned and announced that she always went to bed at eight-thirty.

"I'll drive you and Inocencia home first," he told Sophia when they were in the car.

"Then you'd better take Susan directly to San Miguelito," the old lady said. "Early to bed and early to rise—"

"I will," Armando said, and kissed her cheek.

They drove into the village and when they reached the Rodriquez house both Susan and Armando got out of the car to say good-night to the two ladies. Sophia embraced Susan, and to Armando she said, "Bring Susan to church here some Sunday. Afterward we'll have *comida*." And when Armando hesitated, she said, "Tell her now."

And when he did, Susan smiled and said, "*Gracias*, Doña Sophia. *Me gusta...gustaria...*" She looked helplessly at Armando. "That's as much as my Spanish can manage," she said. Then she turned to Inocencia. "I'll see you on Friday."

"Yes." Inocencia smiled warmly. "Thank you for asking me. And for asking..." She glanced quickly at her mother. "Thank you for asking me," she said again.

Armando took both women to their door and helped them inside. When he returned to the car he frowned at Susan and said, "Why in the world would you do such a thing?"

"What thing?" Susan asked, though she knew very well what he was talking about.

"Why did you tell Inocencia to bring Francisco to dinner?"

"Because it's about time the two of them got together for a date."

"A date? At her age?"

"Yes! She's still an attractive woman, Armando. Francisco has loved her and waited for her all these years, and she hasn't done anything about it because of her family."

"We have our customs," he said coldly. "Francisco is a divorced man—"

"Oh, for heaven's sake!" Susan faced him. "Customs, traditions—"

"Perhaps they don't mean as much to you in your country as they do to us. You're a gringa, you don't understand our ways."

"How dare you say that?" She was so mad she wanted to tweak his nose. "And don't call me a gringa," she snapped.

He clenched the steering wheel and tried to force himself to calm down. "You don't understand our ways, Susana. We're a very proper people."

"Proper or hard-nosed and narrow? There *is* a difference."

"Dammit, Susana..." Armando let out the breath he'd been holding. "I don't want to fight with you," he said.

"I don't want to fight, either. Now please take me home."

Armando started the car, but instead of taking the road to San Miguelito he drove back the way they'd come. "It's late," he said. "You'd better stay at the ranch tonight."

"It's only eight-thirty."

"'Early to bed, early to rise...'" His anger forgotten, Armando grinned and reached for her hand. "I'll take you back in time for your class tomorrow," he said. "Don't be angry."

Susan didn't answer him.

He didn't turn around.

When he parked in front of the patio Susan mumbled under her breath about macho males who thought they could get away with anything, and that by all that was holy she wasn't going to set a foot in his house.

He got out of the car and came around to her side. He gave her his hand. "Come along," he said.

Susan glared at him.

"If you don't come out, I'll get back in the car and we'll make love right here."

"You wouldn't dare!"

"Move over."

Susan looked at him a moment, then with a shake of her head she got out of the car.

Armando took her hand and led her into the house and down the corridor to the room where she had stayed when she'd been ill. He stopped in the doorway and said, "My grandfather told me that he and my grandmother never went to bed while they were still angry. He told her that she could start being angry again in the morning if she wanted to, but that nights were made for love."

He cupped Susan's face between his hands. "My grandfather was a wise man," he said softly. "The night *is* for loving."

He kissed her, and as suddenly as her anger had come, it disappeared. She clung to him, and when he picked her up and carried her into the bedroom she buried her face against his throat.

Armando undressed her, but when he started to undress himself, she said, "No, let me," and he stood silently while she slipped his jacket off his shoulders and unbuttoned his shirt. She kissed his chest, holding his arms so that he wouldn't move.

Shudders ran through him. She licked at his skin and made slow, circular movements around his nipples with her tongue.

"Hurry," he whispered. "Please, Susana..."

"Shh." She nibbled the corners of his mouth and kissed him, long and deep and hard. But when he tried to pull her into his arms she said, "Wait, Armando. Wait, darling."

She had trouble with his silver belt buckle, and though Armando wanted to help her, he made himself stand quietly until she had pulled it through the loops. And when she tugged the zipper down, he thought his body would explode with wanting her.

At last he stood naked before her. With a cry he brought her to him, his hands against her back to bring her close to his arousal. Then he remembered how afraid she had been that night in her house, and he stopped and waited because he didn't want to frighten her. But when she pressed close to him he kissed her, then picked her up and put her in the bed.

They made love slowly and tenderly. Time and again he brought her almost to the peak, but each time he did he retreated, hesitating because he wanted to make this last. Only when she began to move frantically against him, when she uttered small incoherent cries and pleaded for release, did he take her mouth and whisper, "*Si, mi amor.* Now, *mi amor.*"

And when, in that final moment of ecstasy, she cried his name, he thought his heart would burst with loving her. It was only later, when she lay snuggled against his chest, that Armando realized how he had felt in that final moment.

Loving her. He hadn't counted on that.

Chapter Seven

Francisco Gutierez, a tall, distinguished man in his middle sixties, had warm brown eyes and a prominent Spanish nose. He arrived with Inocencia on his arm and a bouquet of yellow chrysanthemums for Susan.

"That's just what I need for a centerpiece," she said when she thanked him. "Please sit down. Armando isn't here yet, but he'll be along soon. Can I get you a glass of sherry or would you prefer white wine?"

"Wine, please."

"And you, Inocencia?"

"Sherry." Armando's aunt sat on a straight-back chair, hands clenched in her lap, obviously ill at ease.

"I like your house," Francisco said politely. "The view is wonderful."

"I'm sorry you missed the sunset. You'll have to come earlier next time."

A tentative smile warmed his face. "Is there anything I can help you with?" he asked.

"Why don't you just relax." Susan smiled at Inocencia. "Would you like to help me with the flowers?" she said.

Inocencia had been relaxed the afternoon at Armando's ranch, but tonight she was tense and uncomfortable. Susan chatted, trying to put her at ease, but when Inocencia remained silent Susan said, "What is it? Is something the matter?"

A flush crept into the older woman's cheeks. "Francisco and I have never gone out this way, to someone's house, I mean. It was kind of you to invite us, Susana, but I'm worried about what Armando will do when he arrives."

"He won't do anything," Susan said firmly, and hoped that was true. She had seen Armando twice this week and he hadn't even mentioned the Friday appointment. Last night she'd said, "Don't forget that Inocencia and Francisco are coming for dinner tomorrow night."

"I don't approve of your asking them," he'd said with a frown.

"That's been fairly obvious."

"They'll be uncomfortable."

"Only if you make them uncomfortable."

"I wouldn't do that. I have nothing against Francisco. He's a decent man and a respected attorney."

"But?"

"He's a divorced man."

There'd been no compromise in Armando's voice, no room for argument. If that was the way he felt about Francisco's having been divorced, how did he feel about her carrying another man's child?

An involvement of any kind had been the farthest thing from her mind when she'd come to Mexico, but she'd met Armando and she'd fallen in love with him. Her body tingled when she thought about him. He had only to touch her hand and she went weak with longing. She didn't understand what had happened to her or why she reacted this way to a man she'd known for so short a time. She and Armando were from different worlds, and yet when they were together she forgot all the reasons why it was impossible, why—

"Susana?"

Startled, Susan looked at Inocencia. "I'm sorry," she said. "I started thinking about you and Francisco and I'm afraid my mind wandered." She reached up into the cupboard and took down a brown-and-gold pot that she had bought in the market a few days ago. She handed it to Inocencia and began to cut the carrots and onions to put in with the roast. "How long have you and Francisco been friends?"

"We met when we were both in our teens. I was sixteen, Francisco was nineteen. We were *novios*, sweethearts. His mother and father knew my family and they were friends. They were fond of me but they had different plans for Francisco."

Inocencia began arranging the yellow flowers in the brown-and-gold pot. "There was a third cousin," she said, "several years older than Francisco. Her family had a neighboring ranch. A marriage was arranged so that the lands could be joined."

"Didn't Francisco have anything to say about it?"

Inocencia shook her head. "Things were different in those days, Susana. Children did as they were told. We are a traditional people, brought up to respect our parents and their wishes." She stopped to pull the excess leaves off one of the flowers. "I was heartbroken when Francisco married Socorro. And the sad thing is that they were as unhappy as I was. The marriage lasted for six years, then Socorro left Francisco and ran off with the man she had wanted to marry."

"And Francisco got the divorce?"

Inocencia nodded. "A year after it was final he came to see my father to ask for my hand. But father refused because Francisco had been married and divorced."

So three people's lives had been ruined, Susan thought. Well, not Socorro's. She had sense enough to end the marriage. "Why didn't you marry him anyway?" Susan asked in a low voice. "Why didn't the two of you just run away?"

"We thought about it." A faint smile softened Inocencia's face. "We even planned how we would do it. But the day before we were going to leave, Papa had a stroke. I was the only daughter in a family of six boys; it was my job to take care of Papa. When he died five years later, my mother was devastated. I couldn't leave her."

So many wasted years. Susan wanted to put her arms around the other woman. Family and tradition. They were imbedded deep in the heart of the Mexican psyche and there was nothing one poor gringa could do to change it.

When Armando arrived thirty minutes later he greeted Susan formally, then he kissed Inocencia's cheek and shook hands with Francisco.

"I'm sorry I'm late," he said. "Is there anything I can do to help?"

"Inocencia's been helping me." Susan indicated the flowers on the coffee table. "Aren't these lovely? Francisco brought them."

Armando's mouth tightened. "Very nice," he muttered.

Because he didn't approve of the situation, he remained coolly polite all through dinner. He had little to say to Susan or to his aunt, and nothing to say to Francisco. When Francisco reached out and covered Inocencia's hand with his own, Armando frowned and Inocencia quickly withdrew her hand.

But it wasn't Inocencia he was angry with, it was Susana. She'd had no right to arrange this dinner party. The situation between Inocencia and Francisco was none of her affair and he would tell her exactly that, as soon as they were alone.

At nine-thirty he looked at his watch and said, "It's getting late."

"I'm going to serve pumpkin pie and coffee," Susan said, "but if you have to leave, we'll understand."

He glowered at her, then said to Inocencia. "Won't Aunt Sophia worry?"

"Mother's sound asleep by now, Armando." She smiled at Susan. "It was so kind of you to ask us tonight, Susana. I've had a lovely time."

"So have I," Susan said. "It's wonderful having company for an evening." She turned to Armando. "I'm sorry you have to leave."

So angry now that he wanted to shake her, Armando tightened his jaw and said, "I'll have a cup of coffee before I go."

He sat down, arms across his chest, his mouth tight, determined to outstay Francisco and Inocencia.

As though sensing his reason for staying, Susan began to draw Francisco out. Where had he studied law? she wanted to know. What kind of law did he practice?

For the first time all evening, Francisco began to open up. He had gone to the University of Guanajuato, he told Susan, where he had majored in archaeology, until, at his family's insistence, he had turned to law.

"But archaeology is my avocation," he told Susan. "I'm especially interested in Egyptian and Mexican archaeology because there are so many similarities between the two ancient cultures. Have you ever been to the Yucatan?"

And when Susan told him she hadn't, he said, "If you cannot go all the way to the Yucatan while you're in Mexico, you should at least see Tula. It's the legendary lost city of the Toltecs and it's less than a three-hour drive from San Miguelito."

"Why don't we go together?" Susan said. "We could pack a picnic lunch and make it an all-day trip."

Francisco's nice brown eyes warmed. He looked appealingly at Inocencia.

"Yes ... yes, that would be lovely," she said.

Armando stiffened. Damn! he thought furiously. What was Susana up to? First she'd invited Tia Inocencia and Francisco to dinner, now she was setting up a foursome for their next date!

"It's difficult for me to get away from the ranch during the day," he snapped.

"That's too bad," Susan said. "But the three of us could go, couldn't we? How about next Friday, Inocencia?"

Armando was almost too angry to speak by the time Francisco and Inocencia left. When they had gone he paced up and down in front of the fireplace. "What in the hell do you think you're doing?" he roared.

"Clearing up the dishes," Susan answered, as she began to gather the dessert plates.

"That's not what I mean and you damn well know it."
Armando ran a hand through his hair. "I told you what
the situation is, what it has been for years between Tía
Inocencia and Francisco. Yet you invited them to din-
ner tonight and now you've arranged an all-day outing.
What in the hell do you think you're doing?"

Hands on her hips, as angry as he was now, Susan
matched his frown with one of her own. "I like your
aunt," she said. "I think it's terrible that she and Francisco have been apart all these years."

"So you've taken it upon yourself to bring them together?"

"I just want Inocencia to have some fun."

"At her age? Really, Susana." He shook his head.
"You don't understand our ways. There are certain
things that are correct and acceptable, and things that
are not. There can be no compromise on the right and
the wrong way, no possible relationship between my aunt
and Francisco."

Susan had begun to stack the plates, but now she
stopped and turned to face him. She held her body
poised, as though for flight, and her face had gone white
and still. "I wonder," she said quietly, "what your
family would think of our relationship."

Armando stared at her.

"I wonder what *you* think of our relationship." And
before he could answer she said, "If you can't accept
Francisco because he was married before, then how can
you accept me? I'm carrying another man's child, Armando. What does that make me? A pariah like Francisco?"

"This has nothing to do with you."

"Doesn't it?" Hands clenched tight to her sides Susan faced him. "We sleep together," she said. "We make

love together. What does that make me in your eyes, Armando? In your particular code of ethics? I'm pregnant and unmarried, and certainly, in your view of things, that is neither proper nor acceptable."

He took a step toward her, but she backed away from him.

"Am I a convenience, Armando? Someone to hold when the nights are cold?"

His face tightened. "You know better than that."

"Do I?" Susan shook her head. "I'm not blaming you for what has happened between us. It was as much my fault as yours. But it can't continue. We both know that there isn't any hope of ... of anything more than what we've had."

He didn't know what to say, but before he could say anything, Susan said, "I think it's better if we don't see each other again, Armando."

"Susana..." He took a deep breath. Perhaps she was right. Perhaps it was better to end whatever it was between them now before it went any further. Steeling himself against the pain the words cost him, he said, "I'm sorry you feel that way." He picked up his jacket and looked at her, then quickly away. "Good night, Susana," he said.

When he had gone she closed the door and stood for a few moments with her back against it. She felt empty inside, bereft, more alone than she'd ever been in her life.

The orange kitten wound itself around her ankles and she bent to pick it up. Then, her face against the softness of fur, she began to cry.

Susan went to church on Sunday morning and although like the time she had gone to Mass with Armando, she understood little of the Spanish, she felt a sense of comfort in being there. As she was leaving Father Ramiro greeted her and said, "Wait until I've said hello to everyone and we'll have breakfast together."

And when he had changed from his cassock to dark trousers and a sweater, they went to the same restaurant overlooking the plaza where they'd had coffee before. He ordered *huevos rancheros* for both of them and while they were waiting for their order to come, he asked her if she'd seen Armando.

"He came for dinner on Friday night," Susan said. "I'd also invited his aunt, Inocencia Rodriquez and her friend, Francisco Gutierez."

"Ay Dios mio." Father Ramiro grinned and crossed himself. "How did you come to do that, muchacha?"

"I met Inocencia at Armando's ranch. She's a lovely woman and I like her. Armando had told me about Francisco, that because he'd once been married and divorced, Inocencia's family wouldn't permit them to marry. I think that's terrible. The woman's sixty-two years old. She could have been married all this time, had children, but because the Church doesn't believe in divorce—" Susan stopped. "Oops," she said. "Sorry. I didn't mean to step on your clerical toes."

"You didn't." Ramiro smiled as the waiter approached with their food, and when they had been served he said, "Actually the Church today is much more sympathetic with cases like Inocencia and Francisco's. There are dispensations. I have no doubt that if they applied for it, an annulment could be arranged." He dropped two sugar cubes into his coffee. "The problem is not so much with the Church as it is with Inocencia's family. They're very strict in—"

"Tradition," Susan said, and made a face.

"Exactly. Armando, although he's a young man, is from the old school in his thinking. I once told him he'd been born a hundred years too late, he should have been a Spanish nobleman or a prince of the Church. His standards, his ideas of what is proper and what is not, are rigid. He's a good man, perhaps the best man I have ever known, but I fear he can be set in his ways." He looked at Susan across the table. "How did he feel about your inviting Inocencia and Francisco to dinner?"

"He was furious." She hesitated, then said, "We quarreled. Not just because I'd invited Inocencia and Francisco to dinner, but because I suggested a day trip to Tula."

"A wonderful place. I haven't been there in years." He spooned *salsa* onto the already spicy *huevos rancheros*. "Has Armando agreed to go along?"

"He hasn't agreed or disagreed, but I don't think he'll go. I don't think I'll see him again."

"Ay, muchacha. I'm sorry. Armando has such strict ideas about right and wrong." His expression thoughtful, he looked out at the square. "Perhaps I shouldn't tell you this," he said at last, "but I'm going to. Several years ago Armando became engaged to a young woman. He broke the engagement shortly before the wedding was to take place. When I asked him—as his friend, not as his priest—why he had done it, he told me that Mercedes had had a love affair with a young man the year before she'd met him."

"The year before...?" Susan stared at Father Ramiro unbelievingly.

Ramiro nodded. "As I said, Armando has rigid ideas."

A terrible sense of hopelessness swept over Susan. If Armando hadn't married because his fiancée had not been a virgin, then how must he feel about her? She pushed her plate aside because she knew if she ate another bite she would be ill.

They chatted a few more minutes, and when they got ready to leave Susan said, "Why don't you come along with us to Tula on Friday?"

"I don't know, Susana. If I go along it's almost as if I'm giving my sanction to Inocencia and Francisco being out in public together."

"I hadn't thought of that. If you don't think it's wise, I'll understand."

"If Sophia finds out she'll be after me like a ninety-year-old tornado," he said with a grin. "But I'll go with you anyway. I say Mass at six and again at eight. What time shall I be ready?"

"Francisco and Inocencia are coming at nine. We can pick you up at the church."

"I hope Armando will decide to come, too." Father Ramiro took Susan's hand. "It's none of my business, muchacha, but I will ask anyway. Are you in love with Armando?"

"No, I'm... I'm fond of him but..." Her voice wobbled. "Yes," she said. "Yes, I think I'm falling in love with him."

"Ay, Dios." With a sigh Father Ramiro said, "On Tuesday I will say a special prayer to Saint Anthony that somehow everything will work out."

Susan tried to smile. "Why Saint Anthony and why on Tuesday?"

"That is the day that all of the single women in San Miguelito go to Mass to pray for a husband." He winked at her. "It does no harm to put in a good word for a friend."

Friday morning dawned bright and beautiful. Inocencia and Francisco arrived a few minutes before nine; Armando came a few minutes later.

He said, "*Buenos dias*, Francisco." He turned to see his aunt coming across the patio. "Good morning, Tia," he said, then stopped, startled. Instead of the conservative clothes she usually wore, his aunt was dressed in a dark green pant suit, a white turtleneck sweater and boots. She looked younger and prettier. But Tia Inocencia in pants?

"Good morning, Armando." Susan's heart did an unexpected flip-flop. To cover her nervousness, she said, "I've invited Father Ramiro to come along with us." She handed Armando the basket of food she had packed for their lunch and tried not to see the look of consternation on all of their faces.

Armando put both Susan's basket and the cooler of food Inocencia had brought into the trunk of his car. He slammed the lid down, then tight-lipped and grim he looked at Susan and asked, "Would you like to drive?"

"No, thank you," she said with an aplomb she didn't feel.

Father Ramiro was waiting on the steps of the church when they arrived. *"Buenos dias,"* he said when Susan got out of the car so that he could sit in front with Armando. "Isn't it a fine day for an outing? And don't you look pretty this morning?" He reached into the back to shake hands with Inocencia and Francisco. "I haven't been to Tula in years," he said. Then he grinned at Armando and said, "Good to see you," and helped Susan into the back seat next to Francisco and Inocencia.

Armando tightened his hands on the steering wheel. He wished he hadn't come. He told himself it was to chaperon his aunt, but he knew the real reason was because he hadn't had a moment's peace since he'd left Susan last Friday night. As difficult as it had been for him to face, he had come to the conclusion that Susan had been right, there really wasn't any hope for them. He'd see her this one more time and that would be the end of it, the end of whatever there might have been.

They reached Tula a little before twelve. The first things Susan saw when they approached the archaeological site were the giant stone statues of the warriors. They dominated the hillside—scarred monoliths built to guard a civilization long since faded into time. She scrambled out of the car, so anxious to see the archaeological wonder that she couldn't wait.

Francisco, as enthusiastic as Susan, began to explain the history of the Toltecs. For over an hour the five of them wandered around the remains of the main ceremonial center of a town where forty thousand people had once lived: the main pyramid, the ball court, the palace and the plaza.

Armando watched Susan. She looked very pretty this morning in white cords and a short-sleeved pink sweater. Her face was tanned from working with the flowers in her patio and glowing with good health. She'd tied her chestnut hair back with a pink ribbon, and that only added to her fresh, young look.

He wanted to touch her, and because he knew that he shouldn't, that if he did he would be lost, he fell a few steps behind the others so that he could watch her without her being aware of him.

When the sun grew hot, they found a place under the trees where they spread a blanket and brought out the picnic lunch. Inocencia, more at ease now, laughed and chatted while she fixed a plate for Father Ramiro.

"Isn't it lovely here?" she said. "I'm so glad we came, Susana."

"Yes, so am I," Susan said with a smile. She was glad that she had suggested this excursion so that the thwarted lovers could spend a day together, yet saddened that Armando so obviously disapproved of them and of her.

As though reading her thoughts, Armando turned and looked at her. For a moment their glances held, then he looked away.

When they finished lunch, Francisco said to Susan and to Inocencia, "Would you like to walk a bit?"

"You two go ahead," Susan said. "I'm too lazy for a walk." She lay back on the blanket and watched the couple as they made their way across the field to the ruins beyond. They were holding hands, and as she watched, Francisco put an arm around Inocencia's waist and Inocencia leaned her head against his shoulder. When they disappeared in the direction of the ball court, Father Ramiro stood up.

"I'm going to have another look around and try to walk off some of my lunch," he said. And with a nod to Armando, and a smile at Susan, he strode off in the direction of the warrior figures.

For a long time neither Armando nor Susan spoke. She lay with her arm across her eyes, pretending to sleep.

"I'm sorry about the other night," Armando said. "What is between Inocencia and Francisco has nothing to do with us, with our relationship. I don't see why we can't go on as we were before, seeing each other—"

"Sleeping with each other." Susan sat up. "I'm not a part-time woman, Armando. I never have been. You've been very kind to me, right from the first day we met, and I'm grateful. But it was a mistake, for both of us, to—"

"Make love?" he asked. And angry again he said, "You were right the other night. We are too different. We come from different worlds. I'm Mexican and—"

"And I'm a pregnant gringa." Susan's smile was bitter. "You don't have to explain, Armando. I understand perfectly."

She got up and dusted off her white cords. "I'm going for a walk," she said, and when Armando started to get up, she said, "There's no need for you to come. I'd like to be alone for a little while."

He stared after her, then slowly got to his feet. He wanted to talk to Ramiro. Maybe if he did he'd get things straight in his own mind.

He found the priest inspecting one of the giant figures. "These never fail to amaze me," Father Ramiro said. "I keep wondering how they did it, those workmen of so long ago. What kind of tools did they use? These figures are almost five meters tall. How did they erect them? I wonder."

He turned to look at Armando. "I'm glad I came today, in spite of the fact that you're behaving like a curmudgeon. Susana's a lovely young woman. She deserves better. She—"

"Armando!"

He swung around. Inocencia came running toward him. "It's Susana," she screamed. "She's fallen. She's unconscious."

He glanced at the priest, then he began to run, his heart racketing in his chest. If anything had happened to Susana... He came up over the rise of the hill and saw her lying at the foot of the pyramid. Francisco knelt beside her.

"What happened?" he asked when he came closer.

"She fell," Francisco said. "Inocencia and I were walking toward her. She was on the fourth or fifth step. We called out and when she saw us she waved and started down. She must have slipped on a loose stone."

Her face was gray. A trickle of blood ran from a wound on her forehead.

"Susana?" Armando knelt beside her. "Susana?"

Her eyelids fluttered.

"What...?" Susan opened her eyes. "What happened?"

"You fell, *querida*." Inocencia wiped the blood away with a white handkerchief. "Are you all right? Do you think anything is broken?"

"No, I..." Susan tried to sit up, but when she did the ground tilted. She closed her eyes and clung to Inocencia's arm.

"We've got to get her to a hospital," Armando said.

"She's had a nasty fall but nothing seems to be broken," Father Ramiro said. "She'll be all right in a minute or two." He put his hand on Armando's arm. "Take it easy, lad, your face has gone as white as hers."

"You don't understand." Armando looked at his friend. "Susana's pregnant."

For a moment there was only stunned silence, then Inocencia said, "Francisco, bring the car around. Hurry!"

Armando picked Susan up. She murmured in pain and he said, "Easy, easy now."

She put an arm protectively across her stomach. "My baby," she whispered. "Armando... Armando, please, don't let anything happen to my baby."

He tightened his arms around her. "I won't," he said.

And then, as quickly as he could without jarring her, he carried her toward the waiting car.

Chapter Eight

Armando paced up and down the hospital corridor. The doctor had been with Susan for almost twenty minutes. If the doctor didn't come out soon he was going in.

Ramiro got up and put a detaining hand on his arm. "Take it easy, Armando. Susan will be all right."

"What in the hell is he doing in there? Why doesn't he come out and tell us something?"

A nurse went by and Armando grabbed her arm. "Look," he said, "the doctor's been in there with Señorita Alexander for a long time. Can you find out what's happening? What—"

The door opened and the doctor came out. Inocencia and Francisco jumped up, but it was Armando the doctor spoke to.

"Are you her husband?" he asked.

"No, I'm . . . I'm a friend."

The doctor hesitated and Armando said, "I know about her pregnancy, doctor. How is she?"

"She had a nasty bump but other than that she seems to be all right. I've given her a light sedative so she's more comfortable now. I'd like to keep her here over-night for observation and when she goes home she should stay in bed for a few days to make sure there are no problems. You can go in now if you want to."

"Gracias a Dios," Inocencia said when the doctor turned away. "Susana can't stay alone, of course. I'll take her home with me."

"You have enough to do taking care of your mother," Armando said. "I'll take Susana to the ranch. Juanita will take care of her."

"While you two are arguing I'm going in to see Susana." Before Armando could answer, Father Ramiro pushed open the door of Susan's room.

"You gave us a scare," he said when he drew up a chair beside the bed. "How are you feeling, muchacha?"

"A little bruised. Kind of foggy." Susan tried to smile. "The doctor gave me an injection. It's making me sleepy."

"He says you're going to be fine." He took her hand. "Right now both Armando and Inocencia are arguing about who you're going home with tomorrow. Inocencia's determined you're going with her, but I have a hunch Armando will win."

Susan shook her head. "I don't want to involve Armando any more than I already have. It's best if I go back to San Miguelito."

"You shouldn't be alone, Susana, not in your condition." The priest hesitated. "How far along are you?"

"A little over four months." Hot color crept into Susan's cheeks. "I'm not married."

"But you want the child, that's what's important, isn't it? The welfare of the child."

"Oh yes." She lay her hands over her stomach.

"Then you must do whatever the doctor says and allow either Inocencia or Armando to take care of you until you're feeling better." He patted her hand. "I'd better go out so they can come in. Take care, Susana, I'll remember you in my prayers."

When he went out, Inocencia and Armando came in. Inocencia sat beside Susan, stroking her hand, but Armando stood at the foot of the bed, a strange expression on his face.

"How do you feel?" he asked.

"Okay. Umm...sleepy. The doctor gave me something."

"Then sleep, my dear," Inocencia said. "We'll be here with you."

Susan looked at Armando. "I'm all right," she murmured. "You don't have to stay."

"I'll stay."

She struggled to keep her eyes open, but when she yawned again she said, "Maybe I'll just...close my eyes for a minute."

Inocencia stroked her hand. "Sleep, muchacha," she said. And Susan closed her eyes.

When she awoke the room was dark except for a single dim light in the far corner. She looked around slowly, trying to remember where she was and why her body hurt. When she turned her head she saw Armando sitting beside her.

"How do you feel?" he asked.

Susan wet her lips. "A little groggy. May I have a glass of water?"

He helped her to sit up and held a glass to her lips. "You gave us a scare," he said.

"I gave myself a scare." She rubbed a hand across her head and felt the bandage. "How long do I have to stay here?"

Armando eased her back down in the bed. "You can leave in the morning. I'm going to take you home with me."

Susan shook her head, but before she could speak Armando said, "I've already had words with Tia Inocencia about this, so don't you argue with me."

"Armando, I—" Tears welled up in Susan's eyes. "This isn't any good for you," she whispered.

He took her hand. "Go back to sleep, Susana."

"You ought to go home and get some rest."

"I'd rather be here."

She looked up at him. "You told them that I'm pregnant, didn't you? You shouldn't have."

"It doesn't matter. All that matters is that you're all right." He smoothed the hair back from her forehead, and at last she closed her eyes and the hand he was holding relaxed in his.

In the dim light of the room Susan looked very small and fragile, the way she had looked this afternoon, crumpled at the foot of the pyramid. For a moment he'd been too terrified to move. Thoughts had skittered around in his head. Fear...and shame because he'd been so cold, so distant all day. And the thought had come, maybe she'll lose the baby.

Armando's eyes smarted with unbidden tears as he silently cursed his meanness of spirit. Susana looked so alone, so vulnerable. She was in a foreign hospital in a country that was not her own. She didn't understand the language. She was alone except for him.

When she murmured in her sleep, he stroked her hand and said, "It's all right. I'm here, Susana." And she quieted.

He had not meant to fall in love with her. She wasn't at all the kind of woman he had pictured himself married to. She wasn't Mexican, nor was she Catholic. She was nothing like Mercedes Lambari.

He had courted Mercedes for almost two years, and during those two years he had never made love to her. For the first year he did little more than hold her hand. Once they became engaged he would kiss her good-night when he took her home. That had been the only intimacy they had shared. And while he hadn't been happy about it, he had accepted it. A bride came to her husband's bed a virgin. That's the way it was meant to be.

But it hadn't been like that with Susana. There had been magic between them almost from the beginning. He had only to look at her, to have her look at him, and his body caught fire. The first time they had made love, it had been unlike anything he'd ever known; it had been fire and ice, lightning flashing across the sky. It had been hunger and a need too urgent to be denied. He'd been too consumed by passion to think of proper or improper.

There had been other women in his life, but with none of them had he felt the way he did with Susana. Making love with her had seemed the most natural, the most wonderful thing he'd ever experienced. If it were not for her pregnancy he would marry her tomorrow.

Armando leaned his head back against the chair and closed his eyes. This was the first time he had admitted to himself that he was in love with Susana, that he wanted to marry her. This was the first time he had allowed the thought to surface, and even now he tried to push it somewhere back into his subconscious, for though he loved her he knew he could not accept her child.

She was too far along to consider an abortion. The next recourse would be for her to have the child and put it up for adoption as soon as it was born. He didn't think Susan would do that, but certainly it would be the best, the logical thing to do. She would have other children, his children. In time she would forget about the first child she had carried.

If only he could convince her that was the best thing to do.

Coming back to the same room at the Rancho La Gloria was almost like coming home for Susan. Juanita hovered over her. She fed her chicken soup, she baked custard and bread pudding and made special herbal teas that she said pregnant women in Mexico drank to be sure they had healthy babies.

Inocencia came every day and she always brought something she had baked, homemade bread or brownies or strawberry tarts. And one day she brought Susan a satin-and-lace nightgown in a delicate shade of pink.

"You're too young to be wearing Juanita's gray flannel," she said.

Susan reached up to hug Inocencia, and when she opened the gaily beribboned box and saw the gown she said, "It's beautiful. I want to put it on right now."

Before Inocencia could stop her she got up and went into the bathroom. And when she came out wearing the gown she said, "I love it, Inocencia. Thank you, and thank you for being so nice to me."

"I like you, Susana. We're friends, yes?"

"Yes." Susan looked shyly at the older woman. Inocencia hadn't mentioned Susan's pregnancy even though she'd known about it since that day in Tula. Now, deciding it had to be talked about, Susan said, "I was afraid after you knew about the baby that you wouldn't want to be friends."

"Now why in the world would you think that?" Inocencia pulled back the sheets and when Susan lay down, she sat on the bed beside her. "If truth were told, Susana, I envy you. I'm even a little jealous of you."

Susan's eyes widened. "Jealous?"

Inocencia nodded. "I've wanted children for as long as I can remember, Susana. That's all I talked about in my teens, how many children I would have and what their names would be." She picked at the crocheted spread. "If I had been more courageous, if Papa hadn't died, if my mother hadn't needed me..." Inocencia sighed. "But things happen in people's lives, Susana. We don't always get what we want."

"It's not too late for you and Francisco."

Inocencia turned away. "It was too late a long time ago."

"I don't believe that. I've seen the way Francisco looks at you. I know he loves you."

"Perhaps he does, Susana, but he no longer speaks of marriage."

"Then why don't you speak of it?"

"Me?" Inocencia looked startled. "Are you saying that I should propose to *him*?"

"Why not? All he can do is say no." Susan smiled. "But I don't think he will."

"Oh, I couldn't." Inocencia blushed. "I mean I—I wouldn't know what to say. And there's my mother to think of. She'd never... I couldn't... Oh, my goodness, I could never do such a thing."

Susan lay back against the pillows. "Couldn't you?" she asked with a grin.

Inocencia's face softened. "You're a wicked girl." She laughed, then her face grew solemn and she said, "I don't know the circumstances of your pregnancy, Susana, but I would guess they aren't altogether happy. But what is important is that you will have a child of your own. That's what matters now."

Susan's eyes flooded with tears. No one had spoken to her like this since she had carried the baby. Zachary had assumed she would have an abortion. Maria, though a friend, had been shocked that she hadn't considered it. And Armando? Her pregnancy embarrassed him, and that hurt worst of all.

When Inocencia left, with the promise that she would return the following day, Susan lay back on the pillows. Dr. Garcia was coming to see her in the morning and if everything was all right, she'd be able to go back to San Miguelito.

Armando had been kind but distant this week she'd been in bed. He left the house every morning to tend to things on the ranch and he rarely returned before dark. He always came to see her after he had bathed and changed his clothes. He told her that he had spoken to Esperanza and that Smooch the cat was all right. He always asked her how she felt and if there was anything she wanted. But it was as though he spoke by rote, as though he were only going through the motions.

That night before he came, Susan went into the bathroom. She bathed, then brushed her hair until it fell softly about her face, and put a pale coral gloss on her lips because she wanted to look nice for Armando. She hoped that tonight he would stay with her for a little while. Perhaps they could eat dinner together here in the room. Perhaps they could recapture a bit of the magic they'd had before.

"Inocencia was here today," she told him when he came. "She brought the gown as a present."

"It's very pretty." Armando glanced at her, then quickly away.

He stayed for a few minutes later, then he told her good-night and left.

And Susan knew that whatever he had felt for her before, he felt no longer.

Dangerous shadows crowded the room. She tried to distinguish shapes, forms. A chair loomed large. The stiff-legged table next to it held a lamp... or was it a lamp? Maybe it was something else. A man's head. A man was hiding behind the table.

She panted with fear. If she could reach the light... She tried, but it was too far away. She couldn't move to reach it and she began to moan in frustration as well as fear.

He came toward her out of the darkness. She tried to scream but there was no sound.

He reached for her. She tried again. This time the scream ripped through the darkness. He put his hands on her. She screamed again. "Go away! Don't touch me! Don't...!"

"Susana!"

"Let me go!"

"It's Armando. I'm here, Susana. Nothing is going to hurt you."

"Armando?"

"Yes, dear."

Susan stared at him, then with a low cry she flung herself into his arms and began to weep, great shuddering sobs that wracked her body.

Armando tightened his arms around her. "It was only a dream," he soothed.

"The same dream," she wept. "Ever since Zac—" She bit down hard on her lip and tried to force herself to calmness. "I'm sorry." She gulped down a sob. "Sorry I awakened you. Sorry I—"

"Don't!" He drew her closer and began to rock her in his arms. "Don't be sorry for anything," he murmured. "It isn't your fault."

Silently then he cursed his unkindness, his coldness. He wanted to protect her, to hold and comfort her. He wanted to tell her that he loved her and that it didn't matter that she carried another man's baby.

But, God help him, it did matter.

When he had soothed her to calmness he lay down beside her. "There'll be no more bad dreams tonight," he whispered. "But if there are, I'll be here with you."

At last, safe in the comfort of his arms, Susan slept.

He was gone when she awoke the next morning.

That afternoon Dr. Garcia came from San Miguelito. He had consulted with the doctor at the hospital in Queretaro, and after examining Susan concurred with the other doctor that there was no cause for alarm. Except for horseback riding or strenuous exercise, Susan could do anything she wanted to do.

"We want to keep an eye on things, though," he said. "I'd like to see you in two weeks."

"Is anything wrong?"

"No, Señorita. I assure you, there is no cause for alarm. But since this is a first baby, I want to be careful."

As soon as he left, Susan went into the bathroom to shower and wash her hair. "I'll have dinner in the dining room with Señor Cobian," she told Juanita.

Armando had come to her room last night. He had held her and soothed her and she had gone back to sleep with him patting her bottom as tenderly as though she were a baby. He still cared about her. Maybe there was a chance that things would work out between them.

The only clothes she had were the ones she'd worn on the day trip to Tula, white cords and a pink sweater. The pants had been torn when she fell, but Juanita had mended and washed them.

"Hmm," Susan murmured when she put the pants on. Juanita must have washed them in hot water. They'd shrunk and now her tummy pooched out... She hesitated, hand over her belly and drew in her breath. Yes, there was an unmistakable bulge; she was beginning to show.

Susan looked sideways at herself in the mirror and a curious sense of pride made her smile. In a little over five months she would have a baby, someone to be responsible for, someone to...

She stared at the bulge and suddenly, unexpectedly, a sense of rage boiled up from deep within her. This moment, this physical realization of the child that grew inside of her, should have been a joyous one. And it would have been if her baby had been conceived by love. Instead it had been created by violence, by a man she loathed.

A hot cauldron of hate boiled to the surface. She stood there, eyes closed, breathing hard, willing her anger to fade. This is my baby, she told herself. It doesn't matter how it was conceived. It's mine, and I will love it.

SILHOUETTE DELIVERS FIRST-CLASS ROMANCE— DIRECT TO YOUR DOOR

Mail the Heart sticker on the postpaid order card today and you'll receive:

— 4 new Silhouette Special Edition® novels—FREE
— a lovely gold-plated chain—FREE
— and a surprise mystery bonus—FREE

But that's not all. You'll also get:

FREE HOME DELIVERY

When you subscribe to Silhouette Special Edition®, the excitement, romance and faraway adventures of these novels can be yours for previewing in the convenience of your own home. Every month we'll deliver 6 new books right to your door. If you decide to keep them, they'll be yours for only $2.74* each —that's 21¢ below the cover price—and there is no extra charge for postage and handling! There is no obligation to buy—you can cancel at any time simply by writing "cancel" on your statement or by returning a shipment of books to us at our cost.

Free Monthly Newsletter

It's the indispensable insider's look at our most popular writers and their upcoming novels. Now you can have a behind-the-scenes look at the fascinating world of Silhouette! It's an added bonus you'll look forward to every month!

Special Extras—FREE

Because our home subscribers are our most valued readers, we'll be sending you additional free gifts from time to time in your monthly book shipments, as a token of our appreciation.

OPEN YOUR MAILBOX TO A WORLD OF LOVE AND ROMANCE EACH MONTH. JUST COMPLETE, DETACH AND MAIL YOUR FREE OFFER CARD TODAY!

Silhouette Special Edition®

FREE-OFFER CARD

4 FREE BOOKS

FREE GOLD-PLATED CHAIN

FREE MYSTERY BONUS

PLACE HEART STICKER HERE

FREE-HOME DELIVERY

FREE FACT-FILLED NEWSLETTER

MORE SURPRISES THROUGHOUT THE YEAR—FREE

YES! Please send me four Silhouette Special Edition® novels, free, along with my free gold-plated chain and my free mystery gift as explained on the opposite page.

235 CIS R1YT
(U-SIL-SE-08/90)

NAME _____

ADDRESS _____ APT. _____

CITY _____ STATE _____

ZIP CODE _____

MAIL THE POSTPAID CARD TODAY!

Remember! To receive your free books, gold-plated chain and mystery gift, return the postpaid card below. But don't delay!

DETACH AND MAIL CARD TODAY!

MAIL THE POSTPAID CARD TODAY!

BUSINESS REPLY CARD

FIRST CLASS MAIL   PERMIT NO. 717   BUFFALO, NY

POSTAGE WILL BE PAID BY ADDRESSEE

SILHOUETTE BOOKS
901 FUHRMANN BLVD
PO BOX 1867
BUFFALO NY 14240-9952

NO POSTAGE
NECESSARY
IF MAILED
IN THE
UNITED STATES

She felt the pooch again, then she tugged the pink sweater down as far as she could over her belly.

Armando looked pleased when he saw her. "Juanita told me you were going to eat with me tonight," he said. "Are you all right? Should you be up?"

Susan nodded. "Dr. Garcia came to see me today. I'm fine now. I can go back to San Miguelito tomorrow."

"Give it another day to make sure." Armando held her chair out and when he had seated her he said, "How does it feel to wear clothes again?"

Susan almost told him about the pooch then, but instead she said, "It's a wonderful relief to be out of bed at last." She picked up the linen napkin and put it across her lap. "I'm sorry I woke you last night, Armando. I must have been screeching like a banshee for you to hear me two rooms away."

"Yes, you were." He frowned. "It must have been a pretty bad nightmare for you to scream that way. Have you always had them? Did you have them when you were a child?"

"No, just since—" Susan looked down at the table. "Just in the last few months," she said.

Armando gripped the stem of his wineglass. Since the rape, he thought. She's had them since the rape.

"You need someone to sleep with you," he said with a slight smile.

"I have Smooch." Her mouth curved with beginning laughter. "He's warm and cuddly and he doesn't snore."

"Neither do I."

Susan stared at him. "Armando, we...we agreed that it would be better for both of us if we—"

"I'm in love with you," he said.

Her eyes went wide with shock.

"I know it's soon. I know I haven't acted like it. But I am in love with you, Susana."

"This isn't the time..." She felt as though she couldn't breathe properly. She shook her head and tried again. "This isn't the time for either of us to fall in love," she managed to say.

"Because of the baby." Armando nodded. "I understand, but I need to know—" He covered her hand with his. "Susana, do you care for me at all?"

She looked at him for a moment, so intently, so searchingly, and it seemed to Armando that when he looked into her amber eyes he could see forever, all of her yesterdays and the promise of her tomorrows.

"Susana?" He waited.

Slowly she nodded. "Yes," she whispered. "Yes, I care for you."

But when he made as though to move toward her, she shook her head. "But I have a responsibility, Armando. I can't think about anything else right now."

"We don't have to decide anything today or next week or even next month. Let me see you through your pregnancy, Susana. Let me help you." He stroked the back of her hand. "At first I didn't understand why you hadn't aborted the pregnancy. I do now and I respect your feelings." He tightened his fingers around hers. "If there were some other way..." He hesitated. "There are so many couples who want to adopt. If you could—"

"No," Susan said. "I couldn't," and with every bit of willpower she possessed, she tried not to show the pain his words caused. "I'm sorry. I understand how you feel, Armando. I don't blame you."

"I love you," he said. "I want to be married to you. But I can't..." She saw the anguish in his face. "I can't accept another man's child, Susana. I'm sorry. I'm sorry as death.''

"So am I, Armando,'' she said. "Oh, so am I.''

Chapter Nine

The next few weeks passed slowly for Susan. She didn't see Armando, but he called occasionally to ask if she was all right or if she needed anything. Their conversations were brief and polite; they had said all that needed to be said.

The pooch in her belly grew larger each day. She had not yet gone into maternity clothes, but had chosen to wear loose blouses and sweaters over a size-larger pants and skirts.

Inocencia and Francisco came often to visit. "At first Mother objected to Francisco's driving me here," Inocencia said, "but I told her you were ill and that was the only way I could get to San Miguelito to see you. She still grumbles about impropriety, but she has not forbidden me to come."

"Have you told her that I'm pregnant?"

Inocencia nodded. "She was shocked at first, but once she got over that, she started knitting. I can assure you of at least half a dozen outfits with matching caps and booties by the time the baby arrives. She wants you to come to Mass with us next Sunday and for the *comida* afterward." Her face broke into a happy smile. "A miracle seems to be happening. Mother has started to accept the fact that I'm seeing Francisco. When I told her it would be awkward if I asked him to pick you up and take you home with us for dinner without inviting him, she said, 'Well, then, of course you must invite him.'"

She hugged Susana. "You've changed things for Francisco and for me," she said. "You're making our lives a bit easier."

"I haven't done very much," Susan said with a shake of her head. "And you can't imagine what your friendship means to me. Especially now."

"Have you heard from Armando?"

"He phones occasionally."

"But you haven't seen him?"

"No, but I understand how he feels, Inocencia."

"Perhaps you do, but I do not. It's not my business, Susana, but I was sure there was something special between the two of you. Armando has known many women, but except for one several years ago, he's never really been serious about any of them. I hoped that in you he had finally met a woman he could love, that he would settle down and marry."

"That would be difficult in my situation. I'm carrying another man's child, Inocencia. That's something that would be difficult for any man to accept."

"I've never asked you, Susana, but I have wondered why you left the man who fathered your child. I mean if it was somebody you thought you loved, couldn't you have worked it out?''

"It wasn't anybody I loved." Susan hesitated, reluctant to tell Inocencia what had happened to her. Armando's aunt was such a gentle woman, as old-worldly and as innocent as her name. How could she understand the violence of rape, the horror of it?

"Susana?" The older woman's eyes were kind. "What is it, *querida*? You can tell me."

Susan took a deep breath. "I was raped," she said. "By someone I knew, an older man, a friend of my family. Love had nothing to do with it."

Inocencia gasped. "What happened to him? Is he in prison or did your family, your brothers, take care of him?"

"I have no brothers." Susan laced her fingers together. "The man was someone I worked with. I was too ashamed, too embarrassed to do anything about it."

Inocencia said something in Spanish, and Francisco, who had been fixing a shelf in Susan's kitchen, came to the doorway and in a shocked voice said, "Inocencia Maria Teresa Rodriquez!"

Inocencia's face flushed. "Go back into the kitchen, Francisco," she said. "This is not a conversation for your ears." And when, with a shake of his head, he retreated, she led Susan to the sofa. "Does Armando know what happened?" she asked.

"Yes, he knows."

"But doesn't he understand that none of this is your fault?"

"He understands, Inocencia, but it's difficult for him."

"Difficult for *him*! *¡Madre de Dios!* What about you?" She clasped Susan's hands in hers. "Are you in love with Armando, Susana?"

Susan nodded. "Yes," she said, "I'm in love with him."

"Then let me talk to him. Perhaps I can—"

"No." Susan shook her head. "It's over, Inocencia. Let it be."

"But—"

"It's over," she said again.

The church in Comonfort was smaller and much less elaborate than Father Ramiro's church in San Miguelito. A three-foot-high white wall, brightened in places by scarlet and purple bougainvillea, enclosed the wide courtyard. Poplar trees grew along the tiled walk leading to the church. There was a look of coolness here, of peace and a soothing calmness.

Susan turned to smile at Francisco and Inocencia. "I'm glad I came," she said. "It's lovely here."

Inocencia and Francisco had picked her up at ten this morning so that they could go to the eleven-fifteen service. "Mama will meet us there," Inocencia had said. Then added, "You look very pretty this morning, Susana."

Susan had chosen the forest-green wool dress because the matching jacket almost disguised the bulge in her belly. But she realized now that at the rate she was growing, this would be the last time she'd be able to wear it before the baby was born.

As they entered the church courtyard they saw Sophia standing at the entrance with a man whose back was turned toward them. And Susan knew, even before he turned, that it was Armando.

For a moment she hesitated, torn between running from the courtyard and running toward him. Then Sophia saw them approaching and raised her arm to beckon imperiously. Armando turned around.

"Ay Dios mio," Inocencia said. "Mama has invited Armando to attend Mass with us." She glanced at Susan. "I'm sorry, I didn't know he would be here."

"It's all right," Susan answered quietly. But the pulse beat hard in her throat and she tightened her hands around her purse.

"Buenos dias, Señora Sophia," Susan said when they drew closer. "Isn't it a lovely day?" She looked up at Armando. "Good morning, Armando."

"Good morning, Susana." He kissed Inocencia's cheek and shook hands with Francisco.

Above them, the church bells began to ring and a flight of mourning doves fluttered against the bright blue sky.

"Let's go in," Sophia said in Spanish. "Last Sunday a group of strangers sat in my pew and I didn't like it. I didn't like it at all." She linked her arm through Armando's and motioned to the others. "Come along, let's not be late."

Armando led the way to a pew near the front of the church. He helped Sophia in, then stepped aside while Inocencia entered. When Francisco hesitated as though to let Susan in, Armando said, "No, you sit next to my aunt."

Then Susan entered and Armando came in beside her. When he knelt down to pray she knelt beside him and he was so totally aware of her that it was all he could do not to reach out and touch her.

Armando closed his eyes and tried to pray, but when he felt the brush of her arm next to his, a sigh trembled through his body and he opened his eyes and looked at her. Her hands were clasped in an attitude of prayer. Her soft hair swept forward, partially covering her face. He couldn't help himself; he put his hand over hers.

She turned and there was an expression on her face, something in her eyes, that clutched at his heart. Just as the old pipe organ in the balcony began to play he whispered, "Susana."

Her lips quivered, but she didn't look away. Armando was held, drowning in the depths of her amber eyes, unable to move until the processional hymn began and everyone stood.

He didn't touch her again, but all through the beginning liturgy he felt her warmth radiating beside him. There was a comfort in being with her again, a rightness and a sense of belonging. Had he been wrong in allowing her to break it off? Should he have insisted that in spite of everything they be married? If he loved her, couldn't he love her child? But what if the child looked like its father instead of like Susan? What if...

So preoccupied was he with thoughts of Susana that he scarcely listened when the priest began the day's homily. He'd missed her these past few weeks with an almost physical ache. The phone calls didn't help, they'd only intensified his longing to see her. Yesterday Tia Sophia had called to invite him to church and to dinner afterward. He had demurred until she said, "I've invited that young American friend of yours."

For a fraction of a second Armando had debated whether or not he should go. He and Susana had agreed not to see each other again. It would be painful for both of them, but he longed to see her.

"...And Christ said, 'Suffer the little children to come unto me, and forbid them not: for as such is the kingdom of God.'"

Armando looked up.

The priest gazed out at the congregation. "I wonder if He spoke only of little children, or if He spoke of us all as His children, for in the following verse He said, 'Whoever shall not receive the kingdom of God with the innocence of a child, he shall not enter therein.' Those words seem to say..."

The innocence of a child. Armando closed his eyes.

He scarcely heard the rest of the homily or the prayer that followed. And when the mass concluded and he stood for the final benediction, he took Susan's hand.

They left the church in two cars; Susana as she had come, with Inocencia and Francisco, Armando with the elderly Sophia.

Susan had never been to Sophia and Inocencia's home before. It was a big, Spanish-style house with high ceilings, polished tile floors partially covered by oriental rugs and classic arched entryways. The furniture was handmade and beautifully carved. Straight-backed chairs with red-velvet seats matched the dark red-velvet drapes.

A feeling of old-world charm and mustiness made Susan feel as though she had stepped back two hundred years into a world of regal elegance.

A uniformed maid served whiskey for the men and sherry for the ladies.

"But not for you, dear," Sophia said as she handed Susan a glass of lemonade. "One must not drink when one is *embarazada*."

"Yes, I know." In spite of herself, Susan felt hot color creep into her cheeks. She wasn't sure what she had expected from Armando's relatives, but this kindly acceptance surprised her.

"That is the way we Mexicans are," Inocencia had explained when Susan questioned Sophia's acceptance of her condition. "At the first announcement of an unmarried pregnancy, the mother of the girl is horrified and the girl is in disgrace. But that is followed by a natural acceptance. There will be a baby in the house again, and everyone loves a baby."

When the conversation turned to local politics, Susan gazed about the room. Several paintings graced the walls, some of them religious, some of quiet pastoral scenes. A bouquet of yellow daisies had been placed on the coffee table that had once been an elegantly carved door. Crocheted doilies covered the arms of the massive chairs. A grand piano at one end held family photographs.

While the others chatted, Susan went closer to see the photos. There were a few young people and children in the pictures, but most of them showed people in old-fashioned clothes and old-fashioned poses. Susan stopped before a wedding picture of a handsome, moustachioed young man and a rather frightened, serious-looking young woman.

"That's Aunt Sophia's wedding picture," Armando said.

The pulse in Susan's throat began its hurried beat again. "She seems frightened, doesn't she?" she said without looking at him.

"Most people are frightened of marriage." He put his hand on her shoulder. "I've missed you, Susana."

"I've missed you, too, Armando."

"I must talk to you."

"Armando, we . . . we've said it all. Talking about it won't help. We—"

"The *comida* is ready," Sophia announced. "Come along now."

"I'll take you home later," Armando said.

Susan shook her head, knowing she should protest because they mustn't start this again. It was too painful for both of them. But even as the protest rose on her lips, Susan hesitated. These last few weeks she had missed Armando so much it hurt. Night after night she'd lain awake thinking about him, longing for him. To start again—and stop again—would only intensify the pain.

They were seated across from each other at a dinner that seemed to go on forever. A cream-of-broccoli soup was followed by a rice-and-shrimp dish, then by chicken in mole sauce and, finally, fresh mangoes sliced over a mango sorbet.

Susan tried to eat, tried to join in the half-English, half-Spanish conversation going on around her, but she was too conscious of Armando's watching her. Time and again their glances met across the table, and there was an expression in his eyes, a hunger and a longing—and something else, something she didn't understand.

When the dinner ended they went back into the *sala*, and Sophia said, "Inocencia, play something for us, will you?"

"Yes, please." Francisco held a chair out for Sophia and said, "Señora?"

The old lady frowned. "My name is Sophia," she snapped. "I've known you since you were in diapers, so you may call me Tia Sophia." Her lips pursed. "Or Mama Sophia, whichever you prefer."

There was a stunned silence. Francisco looked at Inocencia, then back to her mother. *"Gracias,"* he managed to say.

"De nada." Sophia sat down and to Inocencia said, "Play us some Mexican waltzes, my dear."

The others gathered around the piano as Inocencia began to play. The waltzes were unfamiliar to Susan, but she soon found herself humming along with them, and it was all she could do not to start dancing around the room by herself.

Inocencia ended one waltz and began another, and this time the tune was familiar.

Armando put his arm around Susan's waist. *"Cuando escuches este valse,"* he sang softly, "have a memory of me. Think of the kisses of love, that you gave to me, and I gave to you."

Before Susan could protest, he took her hand and led her into the center of the room. "Susana," he breathed against the dark cloud of her hair when he took her in his arms.

She didn't speak because she couldn't. She was in his arms again, if only for a moment, and that was all that mattered. She leaned her head against his shoulder, feeling the rough tweed of his jacket, smelling the wonderful man scent of his aftershave and of him, lost in the music and the warming thrill of his arms around her.

When the waltz ended and yet another began, he said, as he had before, "I'll take you home tonight."

And this time Susan didn't protest.

He held her close to his side all the way back to San Miguelito. They talked of how the day had gone and of Sophia and Inocencia and Francisco, but they didn't speak of all they were feeling.

Susan handed him her key when they got out of his car and started through the patio. She knew that she should say something, that she must not let things start up again between them, but like a somnambulist she let him lead her into the house. He switched on a light, and when he did, Smooch got up from the rug in front of the fireplace. Long and scrawny now in that awkward stage between kittenhood and cathood, he stretched, meowed, then strolled over to Armando and began to weave in and out between his ankles.

"First we light the fire and then we feed the cat," Armando said.

As he began laying the firewood, he remembered the first night he'd ever built a fire for her. They had kissed and afterward he had undressed her in front of the fire. He remembered the shape of her breasts, the curve of her hip, the loveliness of her legs. And the expression of half fear, half excitement when she had looked at his naked body for the first time.

Be careful, he told himself now. You've hurt her before. She's fragile, don't hurt her again.

They went into the kitchen together, and while Susan dished up a helping of food for the cat, Armando set about preparing hot chocolate.

When it was ready he carried the two mugs into the living room and put them on the coffee table in front of the fire.

It seemed right to be sitting here with Susan. A sense of peace settled over Armando as she gazed into the fire, a feeling that this was the way it should always be.

"Remember the first time we sat here?" he said.

Susan looked at him over the rim of the steaming mug. "I remember."

"I wanted you so badly that night. When we started to make love it was all I could do to hold myself back."

He took the mug of chocolate out of Susan's hand. "We went into the bedroom, but when we began to make love again you became frightened. I stopped and I carried you to your bed and I held you."

He touched the side of her face. "That's when I began to fall in love with you, Susana."

"Armando...?" Tears formed and fell slowly down her cheeks.

He wiped them away with his thumb. "My body throbbed with wanting to make love to you," he said softly, "but the need to protect you, to love and care for you was stronger than the physical need." He leaned back against the sofa and drew Susan into his arms. "I've been sad and lonely without you," he said. "You're the first thing I think about when I awaken, and when I close my eyes at night yours is the face I see before I sleep."

For a long moment he didn't speak, and when he did his voice had gone husky with all that he was feeling. "I've been wrong," he said. "I didn't know it until today at Mass."

Susan looked up at him, not understanding.

"The priest spoke of the innocence of a child." Armando drew a long and painful breath. "I've hated your being pregnant. I've hated your child." He shook his head. "How could I have done that to you when I love you?"

"Armando, please." Her voice trembled. "It's all right. I've understood how you felt."

"Have you?" He leaned his face against her hair. He said, "I love you, Susana. I want to marry you. It doesn't matter, about the baby, I mean. I can try..." He struggled for the words, struggled with the uncertainty and the prejudice buried deep inside of him. "Because it's yours it will be all right. I know it will."

Susan knew how difficult this was for Armando. There was a part of her that wanted, without any hesitation, to say, Yes, I'll marry you. Yes, it will be all right. But she had heard that note of uncertainty in his voice and it frightened her. She knew he was trying, and she loved him for that.

She sat up so that she could see him. "I love you so much," she said. "But—"

Armando shook his head. "Don't say no, Susana. Don't say that you won't marry me."

"I wasn't going to say that, Armando." Susan hesitated. "But I want to wait."

"Wait?" His dark eyebrows drew together in a frown.

"Until after the baby is born. Then if you still want to, we will." Susan took his hand. "Less than five months," she said gently. "The beginning of April. That's not too long to wait, is it, Armando?"

"I don't want to wait," he said stubbornly. "I need you, Susana."

"I'll be here for you, Armando."

He looked at her, not understanding.

"We can go on as we were before." She kissed his lips. "That doesn't have to change. Not unless you want it to."

"It isn't what I want." He ran his hand through his hair. "I mean I want it, I want you. Yes, *Dios*, I want you! But I love you and I want to be married to you."

"Marriage can wait for a little while, darling." She kissed him again, and with her lips against his she murmured, "but love needn't wait."

Armando held her away from him, then with a low cry of need he pulled her into his arms.

The bedroom was shadowy in the glow of firelight. As he had that first time, Armando began to undress her. He went slowly. He took the jacket from her shoulders, folded it and placed it over a chair before he turned her around so that he could unzip the forest-green dress. And when she stepped out of it, he placed it over the jacket.

He stood several feet from her, the breath catching in his throat because she was beautiful. In the light of the flames, with the firelight licking at her body, she looked incredibly sexy. The pink lacy bra barely covered her full breasts. The matching garter belt fastened onto sheer lace-topped stockings.

He took a step toward her, dazed by desire. Unfastening her bra, he tossed it aside. Then he unfastened the sheer stockings and slowly rolled them down her legs.

"Step out of your shoes," he said in a voice so low she could barely hear, and when she had, he took her stockings off, then the garter belt. There were only the pink bikini panties now. In a moment she would be naked; she would be his.

Quickly, his gaze never leaving hers, Armando took his clothes off and tossed them aside. He saw her eyes widen, her lips part. He began to slip the panties down her hips, and then he saw it, the slight but unmistakable bulge in her belly. He laid his hand against it. She shivered.

This is her baby, he thought. This is the seed of the man who raped her. He was frozen, unable to move. He felt the warmth of her skin burning into his palm.

"Armando?"

He raised his face and looked at her. With a low cry he brought her into his arms and kissed her with all the fervor and longing and anger in his body. He ground his mouth against hers, trying to wipe away any memory of the other man.

She murmured a protest and he said, "You're mine. You belong to me."

Again, as there had been that first time with him, fear mingled with excitement. His Spanish-green eyes burned into hers, his nostrils flared with passion.

"Armando..." But before she could say anything else he scooped her up in his arms and carried her to the bed. Not even bothering to pull back the heavy blankets he put her down and came up over her.

"I want to hear you say it," he demanded. "Say you love me."

"I love you."

He buried his face against her breasts and drew her close. "I hate it that there was ever anyone but me," he whispered. "I hate the man who hurt you. I hate—"

"Darling," Susan said. "Oh, darling." She stroked the top of his head and slowly, with her gentle touch, she began to ease his anger and his hate. He raised his head and kissed her again, this time gently, tenderly. He kissed her throat and her ears, whispering as he did, "Soon, little love, soon."

He trailed moist caresses down her shoulders to her breasts. He took each swollen peak to gently suckle and when she cried, "Please, Armando, oh, please," he flicked his hot tongue against her rigid nipples.

She'd never known such hunger. Heat burned through her. She reached for him, touched him and stroked him and tried to bring him closer to her frantic body.

He groaned aloud, then with a cry he came up over her and joined his body to hers.

Susan closed her eyes, holding him as he held her, moving as he moved, one with him in this frantic celebration of love. She lavished deep moist kisses against his mouth. She turned her head and tasted the skin of his shoulder. Her body was on fire, she was past all reason, all restraint. She wanted to belong to him, to be one with him, to have him so deep inside her that she would be forever marked by him.

"Yes," she cried. "Oh, yes. Like that, yes."

"Susana?" His voice came harsh against her mouth. "Now?"

His body surged hard against hers, taking her higher and higher. Fire, like the flames reflecting on the ceiling, burned and consumed her. Her body convulsed under his. She cried out and clung to him, heard his answering cry and rejoiced in it.

"Armando," she said over and again. "Armando."

They held each other. He smoothed the sweat-damp hair back from her face and cupping her chin, looked at her in the dimness of the room. "Never deny what is between us," he murmured. "Never deny the magic that is ours." He kissed her. "I love you, Susana. Never forget that."

When the heat of ecstasy cooled they got under the covers. "Let me warm you," Armando said. He curled his body spoon fashion against her back and held her to him, one arm around her waist, his legs pressed close to hers while he rained small kisses on her back.

Susan snuggled and settled against him. He began to stroke her breasts, and his hand moved down to her waist again, then to her belly... And stilled.

Susan waited.

He didn't move his hand.

She felt the sudden tenseness of his body against hers.

He took his hand away. He rested his forehead against her back, but he didn't speak.

"A-Armando?" His name trembled on her lips.

When he didn't answer, the warmth seeped out of Susan's body. She felt cold now, cold and sad and more alone than she'd ever felt in her life.

"It's late," he said. "Go to sleep."

She closed her eyes and when the tears came, she lay very still so that Armando wouldn't know that she was crying.

Chapter Ten

On Christmas Eve the temperature dropped into the forties. Because of the cold and because she wanted something festive for the occasion, Susan wore a dark red velvet dress with long sleeves and a rounded neckline. It was tucked above her bosom and fell, full and fairly concealing, over her five-and-a-half-month-size stomach.

She pulled the heavy wool poncho closer and tucked her hand into Armando's when they left her house and started out to his car. The night was cold and clear and overhead a thin slice of moon rose over the mountains.

Susan stopped for a moment to look up at the Christmas sky. "Isn't it a beautiful night?" she whispered. "I've never seen so many stars."

Armando looked at her instead of at the sky. If anything, Susan had grown more beautiful these last few weeks. Her eyes were clear and her face glowed in pink-

and-white perfection. If it hadn't been for her growing stomach . . . He stopped the thought. That was unworthy of him and unfair to her. Susan was beautiful. Period.

Because he loved her, and because he was ashamed of his thoughts, he cupped her face between his hands and gently kissed her.

"Merry Christmas, Susana," he said when the kiss ended, and he brushed his fingers across her cool cheeks.

"Merry Christmas, Armando." She smiled up at him. "I'm so glad I'm here with you."

"So am I, love." He looked at her for a long moment, then he took her hand and they crossed the patio to the street.

Last night Armando had suggested that they go to ten o'clock Mass at Father Ramiro's church in San Miguelito and from there drive to the ranch to celebrate Christmas Eve with his family. Now as they started toward Armando's car, they heard singing and saw a small crowd gathered a few doors down from Susan's. "Come on," Armando said, "I want you to see this."

As they drew closer he said, "The *posadas* are a Christmas tradition in Mexico, especially in the smaller towns." He put his hands on her shoulders, urging her closer so that she could see.

Near the door of the house, Susan saw a little girl on a burro. She was dressed in pale blue, with a blue *rebozo* covering her hair and her shoulders. Beside her, leading the burro, was a five-year-old, moustachioed Joseph. Staff in his hand and a straw hat on his head, he was dressed in long pants and a brightly-colored Mexican shirt. A small dark-skinned angel in a white dress, with a wobbly halo bobbing uncertainly above her head, stood next to the little boy.

"The children represent Joseph and Mary," Armando said in a low voice. "The people with them are singing to the occupants of the house to open their door because Mary is with child and she and Joseph have no place to stay. The people inside reply by singing there is no room at the inn."

Off-key sopranos, a few baritones and childish voices joined in an enthusiastic chorus, entreating entry. The people inside sang back their refusal, until finally the door swung open and a chorus of voices sang out, "Come in. Come in."

"We could go in if you want to," Armando said. "Everyone is welcome. They'll serve hot punch and cookies and have a piñata for the children." He glanced at his watch. "But we'll only be able to stay for a minute."

"No, that's all right, we'd better go." Susan smiled up at him. "It's a lovely custom, isn't it?"

"Yes, it is." They were alone on the street now, so he kissed her again.

Susan's cheeks were red from the cold and her hair curled softly around her face. And he knew as he helped her into his car for the short drive into town that he had never before, and would never again, love anyone the way he loved her.

The church was crowded by the time they arrived but they found seats near the back beside a family with three boys, a girl and a small baby. The baby cried all through the liturgy but went happily to sleep in his mother's arms when the organ started to play.

The scent of incense and roses mingled with the smell of wax dripping from altar candles. The choir in the loft began to sing Handel's Messiah...

"For unto us a child is born.
    For unto us a son is given."

Susan looked at the sleeping child in the arms of the woman beside her. Baby fists were curled against his face. His cherub mouth looked sweet and vulnerable.

Next Christmas she would be holding her own child in her arms. Joy surged through Susan. A child of her own. What a wonderful feeling those words brought. With all her heart she wanted to share this moment with Armando, but when she looked at him, so silent and solemn beside her, she knew that she couldn't. He wasn't her husband; he wasn't the father of her child. As much as he loved her, she knew he wouldn't understand.

It was after eleven when Susan and Armando left the church and started for the ranch. Still brimming with the joy of what she'd experienced in church, Susan moved closer and said, "This is one of the nicest Christmases I've ever had."

"It is for me, too." Armando brought her hand to his lips and kissed it.

The drive leading up to the ranch house was illuminated with candles that glowed inside paper bags. "This is another tradition," Armando said. "The bags are filled with sand and the candles are stuck into it. Don't ask me why the bags don't catch fire, but they never do."

Christmas lights had been strung above the Spanish arches of the ranch, and from inside Susan could hear the sound of Christmas carols coming from Armando's stereo system.

Inside, the house had been decorated with bright red poinsettias and dozens of flickering candles. One red stocking hung over the big stone fireplace, and a crèche had been arranged on a table in one corner of the room. In another corner there was a Christmas tree.

"Christmas trees aren't part of our traditional holiday," Inocencia said when she greeted Susan. "But Armando wanted to have one for you so that you would feel at home."

Susan turned to look at Armando. It was a thoughtful thing for him to have done and she loved him for it. It brought back memories of other Christmases with her own family, of a house filled with the smell of fresh-baked cookies and hot cider, of cold Christmas mornings when the snow crunched under your feet on your way to church. Of turkey roasting in the oven and pumpkin pies cooling on the counter.

The tree in the corner brought it all back to her, and for a moment her eyes flooded with tears for bygone days and for the mother and father she had loved so dearly.

Armando put his arm around her. "Don't be unhappy," he said.

"I'm not. I'm just remembering." She managed a smile. "And thinking how glad I am to be here with you... with all of you."

Hugs and kisses and greetings of *Feliz Navidad*, Merry Christmas, were said then and they toasted the holiday with hot spiced punch. Until Sophia, sitting in a rocker by the fire said, "Isn't it time we exchanged our gifts?"

Susan handed the elderly lady a gaily wrapped package from the stack she and Armando had brought in from the car. Sophia opened it, careful not to tear the paper, and when she lifted the tissue aside she said, "Oh, it's lovely, my dear. Thank you." She held up the deep rose, fringed shawl that Susan had bought in Queretaro.

Susan's gift to Armando was a pair of silver spurs intricately engraved with Aztec symbols.

"They're beautiful," he said enthusiastically, and immediately put them on the mantle over the fireplace before he handed her a small oblong package.

Inside was a gold watch, its face surrounded by tiny diamonds. Susan held it up for the others to see. "I love it," she said, and kissed Armando's cheek when he fastened it around her wrist.

The other presents were exchanged then, and there were more presents for Susan: a handmade white sweater from Sophia, gold loop earrings from Inocencia, a bottle of perfume from Francisco. But it wasn't the presents that warmed Susan, it was the love and the friendship these people offered her. They had taken her into their hearts and let her share this Christmas holiday with them. She would never forget it or them.

When all of the presents had been opened, they went in to the dining room for the Christmas supper and gathered around the table and held hands while Sophia said grace. Then the kitchen door opened and Juanita, with a cousin she had brought in to help, began bringing in the food.

There wasn't the turkey and dressing, mashed potatoes and giblet gravy and cranberry sauce that Susan was used to. Instead there was *bacalao*, salted codfish cooked in tomato sauce with olives, pimentos and potatoes; spicy roast pork; corn tamales, vegetables and *bolillos*. For dessert Juanita served dried fruits and sugared fritters called *buñuelos*.

"Sometimes we also have turkey or chicken," Inocencia told Susan, "but this year mother asked for a more traditional dinner. I hope you like it."

"I do," Susan said, for while it was indeed different everything was delicious.

The five of them lingered at the table until almost two in the morning. Finally Sophia yawned and said, "If I don't go to bed soon I'm going to fall asleep in the rocking chair."

After she and Inocencia and Francisco left, Susan said, "I haven't had a Christmas Eve like this since I was a child, Armando. I love your family. I feel as though I've always known them."

"They love you, too, Susana." He put another tape on. "It's late. You must be tired."

Susan nodded. "I feel as though I'd like to sleep for a week. Do we have to get up early tomorrow?"

"No, love, you can sleep as late as you like." He took her hand and led her over to the sofa. When she sat down, he swung her legs up and took her shoes off.

In the background Placido Domingo began to sing *"Adeste Fideles."* Susan closed her eyes and when Armando began to rub her feet, she murmured, "That's wonderful. Don't stop." She scrunched farther down in the sofa, then afraid that she'd go to sleep, she opened her eyes. "This is such a comfortable room, Armando," she said, and indicating the portrait of a distinguished looking man above the fireplace, asked, "Is that your father?"

He nodded. "His name was Armando, too. It's pretty much of a custom here in Mexico to name the first-born son after the father." He looked up at the portrait of his father, who had been named after *his* father, and he thought of the child that Susan carried. The family name must be reserved for his child, but what if Susan expected, or wanted, to name her baby after him?

He leaned his head back against the sofa. It was all so complicated. By this time next year the baby would be almost eight months old. How would it change things between Susan and him? How would he feel when she held another man's baby in her arms? And because that made him feel mean and small, he said, "I have another present for you. I wanted to give it to you when we were alone."

He got up and went over to the fireplace and took down the red stocking hanging there. "Merry Christmas," he said when he handed it to her.

"But you've already given me the watch..." Her amber eyes wide with anticipation, Susan reached into the stocking and took out a small blue velvet ring box. She looked at Armando and suddenly her heart began to beat fast against her ribs. Was it an engagement ring? She'd told him she didn't want to talk about marriage until after the baby came, but the prospect of a ring excited her. If he insisted they be married soon, perhaps she'd reconsider. Perhaps she'd...

She opened the box. The Baroque pearl, as large as Susan's thumbnail, was set in an intricate gold mounting. So beautiful that it took Susan's breath away, she was speechless until Armando said, "Do you like it, Susana?"

"It's the most beautiful ring I've ever seen."

He reached for her right hand and slipped the ring on her finger. "It's a promise ring," he said.

She felt a stab of disappointment. The ring was beautiful and obviously expensive. And yet...

She made herself smile and say, "Thank you, Armando. It's beautiful. I love it."

"The promise of tomorrow." He brought her hand to his lips and kissed it.

"Yes," she said. "The promise of tomorrow."

The next few weeks were happy ones for Susan. Six months pregnant now, she fairly bloomed with health. She still walked the more than a mile to her Spanish classes every day, and if she hadn't shopped for groceries, she walked back up the hill to the house. Dr. Garcia had told her that everything was fine, and he confirmed that the baby would be born in the first week in April.

She saw Armando several times a week. He was as kind and as loving as he had always been, and if there was a reserve about him when she spoke of the baby, she told herself she understood how he felt and that he was doing the best he could under the circumstances.

He tried to get her to move out to the ranch. "You won't have to cook or clean or wash clothes—"

"I don't do much of that now," Susan had said with a smile. "Esperanza does most of the work."

"I worry that you're so far from town."

"Only a little over a mile, Armando. Dr. Garcia says the walk is good for me. Besides, my Spanish is coming along fairly well now. I'd hate to give it up."

"I'll teach you."

Susan's eyes twinkled. "You teach me bedroom Spanish. *Amor de mi vida, mi alma, yo te adoro.* Love of my life, my soul, I adore you. That's wonderful, but I can't really use it when I'm shopping for onions."

He brought the subject up again that night when he said, "If you won't come out to the ranch with me, why don't you consider moving in with Inocencia and Sophia? They both want you to. You get on well with Inocencia, and you bring out all of Sophia's motherly instincts."

"She's not nearly as fierce as she seems, is she? At the rate she's knitting baby clothes I should have twins. She and Inocencia and I drove into Queretaro last week to shop for maternity clothes. This is one of the dresses I bought. Do you like it?"

The dress, navy blue with a white collar and cuffs, seemed to make her look more pregnant than she was, Armando thought with a dismay he tried to hide.

"Nice," he said, and began to help her on with her coat.

Armando hadn't done more than glance at the dress and that made her feel sad because she wanted to look pretty for him. But it was a maternity dress, and it hadn't pleased him.

To hide her disappointment, she said, "A new restaurant has opened up here in San Miguelito. I'd like to try it some time."

"New restaurants come and go," Armando said, dismissing the idea.

That was the second time Susan had suggested they dine in San Miguelito rather than drive the fifteen or twenty miles to another town. But whenever she did, Armando always said, "No, let's go to Queretaro." Or Celaya or San Juan. Anywhere but San Miguelito.

And although Susan knew why he preferred to dine out of town where no one knew him, she never spoke of it.

The restaurant Armando had chosen tonight sat on a hill overlooking the picturesque city of Guanajuato that had once produced twenty percent of the world's silver. Steeped in colonial history, with subterranean passages and winding streets, some almost too narrow and sloping for two people to pass abreast, Guanajuato was a place unlike any other, old-worldly, charming and mysterious.

They had eaten there before and the maitre d' greeted them and said, "I have a table by the window, Señor Cobian. Please follow me."

They were halfway across the room when someone called out, "Armando! Is that you?"

And when Armando hesitated, the man pushed back his chair and got up. "It's been a year or two, hasn't it? How have you been?" He turned to the woman sitting with him. "You remember Armando Cobian, don't you?"

"Yes, of course I do." The woman, a stunning brunette with the most perfect skin Susan had ever seen, offered her hand to Armando and smiled at Susan. "Is this your wife?" she asked.

"No," he said a bit too quickly. "Miss Alexander is a friend . . . from Texas. Susan, I'd like you to meet Cesar and Mirna Duran. Cesar and I went to school together."

"Right here in Guanajuato, as a matter of fact," Duran said. "That was before he went to Texas. We both studied law and we both have degrees. Only I have clients and Armando has horses. I sometimes think he has the better of it."

"I know I have the better of it." Armando tightened his hold on Susan's elbow. "We mustn't keep you from your dinner," he said.

"We've only just ordered. Won't you join us?"

"Yes, please," Mirna Duran said.

"Well, we—"

"It's been a long time since we've had a chance to visit." Duran motioned to the maitre d' before Armando could object. "Señor Cobian and his friend will dine with us," he said, and held a chair out for Susan.

She looked at Armando. A muscle in his jaw tightened and flexed, but he said, "*Gracias*, Cesar," and drew up a chair across the table from Susan.

"Did you know Armando when he went to school in Texas?" Señora Duran asked.

"No, we . . . we met here."

"Is your husband with you, or is he back in Texas?"

"He . . ." Susan reached for her napkin and folded it across her lap. "Actually he—"

"Susan's husband is dead," Armando said. "He was killed in an accident four months ago."

"Oh, my dear." Mirna patted Susan's hand. "How dreadful for you."

"Yes." She looked across the table at Armando.

The Durans were nice people and Susan liked them. But she was uncomfortable because Armando was uncomfortable. And because he had lied. She realized that trying to explain her situation would have been awkward for him, but she wished he hadn't lied.

Susan had no idea what she ordered. She poked the food on her plate around and pretended to eat, but the few bites she took stuck in her throat.

She had little to say when they left the Durans. Mirna Duran kissed both her cheeks, and Cesar said, "The four of us must get together soon."

But Susan knew that they wouldn't see the Durans.

"They're nice people," she said cautiously once in the car.

Armando nodded.

"Do they live here in Guanajuato?"

"Uh-huh."

Susan leaned her head back against the seat. "You were embarrassed tonight because of my pregnancy, weren't you, Armando?"

"No, of course not." He turned the radio on and busied himself adjusting it to a music station.

"You were uncomfortable at dinner."

"I wasn't uncomfortable. I'd rather have been alone with you, that's all."

Susan closed her eyes and tried to will away her pain, but she felt so empty, so strangely alien and alone. She knew how difficult it was for him to explain that she wasn't married. But she'd hated his explanation that her imaginary husband had been killed in an accident.

They had little to say to each other on the ride from Guanajuato other than to make an occasional remark about how cold the weather had turned or to comment on the music. Susan wanted to say, Let's talk about it. Tell me how you feel. I'll understand. But she said nothing.

She told herself that Armando had been doing the very best he could to handle what must be all sorts of conflicting emotions about her pregnancy. She tried to understand how difficult this must be for him, but it was difficult for her too.

A few days ago, just after they had gone to bed she'd said, "Armando! The baby's moving. I can feel it."

And wanting to share this moment with him, she'd taken his hand and placed it on her stomach. "There," she'd said, "can you feel it? Isn't it wonderful?"

He'd pulled his hand away. "I don't feel anything," he'd said.

For the past week or two, because Armando had been afraid he might hurt her, they had made love with her astride his hips. The first time he had been constrained, uneasy. Finally he had said, "The room is cold, Susana, you'd better wear a gown." And she had known he hadn't wanted to see her stomach.

Tonight when they returned to her house, Susan tried to quell the edge of anger she'd felt earlier in the restaurant. While she undressed, Armando heated warm milk for both her and Smooch the cat. She drank her milk in bed while he undressed, and when he had finished she said, "Hurry up, I'm freezing in here alone."

When he smiled down at her, the edge of tension ebbed. He came into bed beside her. He held her and warmed her, and in a little while they made love.

But there was a subtle, an almost imperceptible difference in Armando's lovemaking. For though he was as passionately tender as always, in a way she could not define, he seemed to have distanced himself from her.

In that final moment of fulfillment Susan collapsed over him, gasping with pleasure as she murmured his name, her body still quivering with intense gratification, wanting to be as close to him as she could get.

He shifted, as though uncomfortable. "Come lie beside me," he said.

Susan stiffened. He doesn't like the feel of my body, she thought with a terrible sinking feeling. He hates my bigness, my bulge. He hates my being pregnant.

Without a word she lay down beside him and turned her back. He curled against her.

But in spite of his warmth, Susan remained cold for a very long time.

Father Ramiro held his golf club poised over the ball. He took a practice swing, then with a waggle of his hips he drew the club back and swung at the ball. It arched high into the cloudless sky, arced down and rolled to the edge of the green.

"Good shot," Armando said.

"Yes, it was." Ramiro looked pleased. "Let's see you top that."

"Piece of cake." Armando placed his ball on the tee, flexed his shoulders and took a swing. The ball fell far short of his friend's.

"Mind's not on your game," Ramiro said.

"I'm just a little rusty. I need to get out on the course more."

"You're busy at the ranch." Ramiro hesitated. "And I suppose you're seeing quite a bit of Susan."

Armando nodded. "Quite a bit."

"Things getting serious between you?"

"You could say that. I've asked her to marry me."

"I see."

"Is that all you've got to say?"

"No."

They started across the green toward where the white balls lay.

"I wanted to get married now," Armando said. "But Susan insists we wait until after the baby is born."

For a few moments Ramiro didn't speak. But at last he said, "Susan's a lovely woman, Armando. I'm fond of her."

Armando stopped. "I'm waiting for the word *but* to drop."

The priest shook his head. "All right, Armando. Susan is a lovely girl, but what do you really know about her? About her background? Her family? Have you considered the fact that you're very different people? Susan isn't Catholic, nor is she Mexican. She's been raised in a different culture than you have, there'll be things about her you'll never be able to understand.''

Ramiro put his hand on Armando's shoulder. "I'm talking to you as your priest now, as well as your friend. Susan's going to have a baby by another man. Are you sure you can cope with that? How do you know that somewhere in the years ahead you won't resent the child?''

"I won't.'' Armando looked out over the green. "It will be Susan's baby.''

"And yours.''

Armando looked startled.

"Susan will expect you to adopt it, and rightly so. It will have your name. Have you thought about that?''

Armando's eyebrows drew together in a frown. "No, I haven't.'' He swung hard at the grass with his club. "I love her,'' he said.

"I know you do.'' Father Ramiro sighed. "Life doesn't always work out the way we want it to, does it?'' And when Armando didn't answer, he said, "I'm sorry, Mando. Sorry for both of you.''

On the Sunday after the golf game, Armando and Susan, together with Inocencia and Francisco, drove down to the lake for a picnic. Armando acted more cordial toward Francisco now, and although he voiced to Susan his disapproval of any possible engagement between his aunt and Francisco, he found that he liked Francisco more all the time.

The man was obviously devoted to his aunt, and she seemed to take such pleasure in being with him that it was hard for Armando to object whenever Susan suggested they do something with the other couple.

The nights and the mornings were cold, but during the day the temperature rose into the high sixties. Today the sun was shining and the few clouds in the blue sky were as white and fluffy as cotton candy.

Armando and Francisco had brought fishing poles and after they had eaten, the two men walked down to the lake and cast their lines out.

"They're getting along well, aren't they?" Inocencia said.

"And your mother seems to have accepted your relationship." Susan smiled at her friend. "So, what are you waiting for?"

"What do you mean?"

"I don't think anybody would have a fit now if you and Francisco got married."

Inocencia blushed pink.

"Are you afraid of marriage?" Susan asked gently. "I mean because you've never, uh, never been married. Is that it, Inocencia?"

"No, I..." The blush of pink became scarlet.

"It will be all right. If you and Francisco love each other the—the physical part will come naturally."

"I know." The older woman looked down at her hands.

"When you love someone it's so wonderful, so..." She looked at Inocencia. "You know?" she whispered.

"*Ay Dios mio*, I never thought I'd tell anyone."

"Tell anyone what?"

"Francisco and I have been lovers for almost forty years, Susana."

Almost too surprised to speak, Susan could only look at the older woman. "How...?" she squeaked. "I mean where? Without anyone knowing? How did you ever get away from your mother?"

"You've heard about my Thursday night ladies' club?"

Susan nodded.

"There isn't any ladies' club. There never has been."

"So you and Francisco . . . all these years . . . ?"

"Yes, Susana. For all these years we have driven to our small house in Celaya every Thursday. We spend the hours from six to midnight together. Then we go home in our respective cars."

"You have a house?"

"We bought it a long time ago." Inocencia touched Susan's hand. "You look so shocked. I shouldn't have told you."

"I'm not shocked, I'm surprised." Susan hesitated. "And maybe just a little sad."

"Sad? But why, Susana?"

"Because you should have been together all these years. You should be together now." She looked out to where the two men were fishing. "I wish you were married."

Inocencia plucked at a blade of grass. "Francisco proposed to me many times over the last years, Susana. But now he has stopped proposing."

"I've already told you this, but I'm going to tell you again. Maybe it's time you asked him."

"But I—"

"Why don't you, Inocencia? Right now. Today. If he says no, I'll help you push him in the lake."

Inocencia looked uncertain, but a slight smile curved the corners of her mouth.

"Tell Armando that I left my sweater in the car and that I'd like him to get it for me." Susan gave Inocencia a gentle shove. "It'll be all right," she said. "Go on now."

Inocencia pushed herself away from the tree she'd been leaning against. "I'm scared," she said.

"I know."

"Will you really help me push him in the lake if he says no?"

Susan laughed. "You can count on it," she said.

She watched the older woman go down to the lake. She saw Inocencia say something to Armando. He handed her his fishing pole and started in the direction of the car.

Inocencia stood looking out at the lake, and it seemed to Susan that even from this distance she could see the other woman square her shoulders. Then she put down the fishing pole and turned to Francisco.

"Here's your sweater," Armando said to Susan. "I thought you'd be warm enough here in the sun." He draped it across her shoulders. "Feeling all right?"

"Yes, I'm fine."

"The fishing's not any good today. We're not catching anything."

"Aren't you?" Susan asked with a smile. She looked toward the lake. Francisco had dropped his pole. He'd grasped Inocencia's hands. Then he held her away from him for a moment and with a look of absolute joy, he pulled her into his arms.

"What's going on?" Armando asked.

"Your aunt has just asked Francisco to marry her," Susan said triumphantly. "And from the look of the clinch I'd say that he accepted." There were tears in her eyes, but they were happy tears.

"She asked him to..." Armando looked stunned. "But women don't—"

"Some women do."

He frowned. "You put her up to this, didn't you?"

"Yep."

"Dammit, Susana, I—"

"Shh," she cautioned. "Here they come." She took his hand. "Please, Armando, be happy for them."

He glared at Susan, but as his aunt came closer and he saw her face, his own face softened, for it seemed to him as though Inocencia had never been so beautiful.

"We have something to tell you," she said.

Francisco cleared his throat. "Inocencia and I..." He reached for her hand. "We have decided that even though the family disapproves, we are going to be married." He looked at Armando as though expecting an argument.

Susan darted a look at Armando and held her breath.

"I..." Armando looked from Francisco to Inocencia, then back to Francisco. "I think it's time my aunt had the happiness she deserves," he said, and put his hand out. "Congratulations, Francisco. You're getting a wonderful woman."

He kissed Inocencia then. "I'm happy for you, Tia," he said.

Susan hugged Francisco, then Inocencia. "I knew he wouldn't say no," she whispered. Then both women burst into tears.

Francisco and Armando looked at each other helplessly, and when the two women laughed and dried their tears, Armando said, "Have you set a date yet?"

Francisco shook his head. "I petitioned the church for an annulment years ago, but when Inocencia kept putting me off I didn't pursue the matter. I'll have to discuss it with Father Ramiro. We'll have the civil wedding as soon as possible, and I would hope we can have the religious ceremony in the spring." He clasped Inocencia's hand. "We've dreamed of a church wedding for years, now it will be a reality. Our union will be sanctified in the eyes of God."

Armando's head was spinning. He couldn't believe that after all these years his sixty-two-year-old aunt was actually going to marry the man she had loved for so long. And it was Susan, Susan the gringa, who had been instrumental in making it possible. She had brought them together as a couple, in spite of him, in spite of Sophia.

"Will you be my witness?" Inocencia asked Susan.

"I'd love to. Thank you for asking me."

Francisco looked at Armando. "I—I don't suppose you..."

"I'd be happy to," Armando said.

They drank a toast then, three of them with wine, Susan with fruit juice. And as they toasted the lovers, Armando looked at Susan over the rim of his glass.

With a clutch of anguish he thought back to his conversation with Ramiro. His friend had raised so many questions about Susana not being Catholic or Mexican. About her having been raised in a culture different from his own. He had told himself that those things didn't matter, not if he and Susana truly loved each other.

But what about the child she carried? Would Susana expect him to adopt it, to give another man's child his name?

These were things they needed to talk about, but God help him, he didn't have the courage to face her with his doubts.

Chapter Eleven

The civil ceremony took place at the Rancho La Gloria the second week of January. Only two of Inocencia's brothers and their wives came. "Alberto has promised he will come for the church ceremony in March," one of them said, "but Julian, Leandro and Jorge had to work."

"They wouldn't come because they don't approve," Inocencia told Susan. "That makes me a little sad, but the problem is their's, not mine. They married who they wanted to marry, and at last I have the courage to marry who *I* want to marry. I should have done it years ago, but better late than never."

They were in the room that Susan used whenever she stayed at the ranch, and now Inocencia summoned a smile. "How do I look?" she asked.

"Beautiful and bridelike," Susan said.

And it was true. Dressed in a pale blue suit with a matching wide-brimmed hat and blue pumps, Inocencia looked, Susan thought, the very picture of a happy bride.

"I'm so happy," Inocencia said. "At last Francisco and I will be together."

"Where are you going to live?"

"With mother for a little while. Francisco is trying to sell the house in Celaya, and when he does we'll use the money to buy a house here."

"Your mother will miss you."

"San Miguelito is a small town. I'll still see her every day." Inocencia looked at herself in the full-length mirror. "Do I really look all right?" she asked anxiously.

"You look beautiful." Susan hugged her.

Inocencia shook her head. "I can't believe this is happening," she said. "It wouldn't have without your help, Susana. You're the one who gave me the courage to begin seeing Francisco in public, the one who made me propose to him." She took a deep breath. "I think I'm ready," she said.

The others, along with the judge who would marry them, waited in the flower-filled patio. Water bubbled from the old stone fountain, the sun was shining and the day was bright and clear. Francisco looked nervous but eager as Inocencia approached clutching her bouquet of forget-me-nots.

The mother of the bride, wearing a pink dress a shade lighter than Susan's, kissed Inocencia and said, "You look lovely, my dear."

With Susan a step behind her, Inocencia took Francisco's arm and the ceremony began.

Armando, standing to the right of Francisco, listened to the words, but he watched Susan. Her pregnancy was showing now, and she held the bouquet of pink carnations so that they partially hid her swollen stomach.

He had seen Inocencia's two brothers and the other guests' questioning looks when he'd introduced them to Susan. No one had asked about her pregnancy and he wondered as he watched her if they assumed the child was his. He wasn't sure how he felt about that.

When the ceremony was over and Inocencia and Francisco were man and wife in the eyes of the state if not in the eyes of the church, Armando embraced his aunt and shook hands with Francisco. "Congratulations," he said. "I hope you'll always be as happy as you are today."

And Francisco answered, "I have waited all my life for Inocencia. Now that we're finally together, I know we'll be happy."

A reception followed the civil wedding. Champagne glasses were raised to toast the bride and groom, and the table fairly groaned with food. At one end of the patio a mariachi group began to play. The bride and groom danced, then the judge who had married them, a portly red-faced gentleman in his seventies, asked Susan to dance.

When finally everyone had gathered at the long table, one of Inocencia's sisters-in-law turned to Susan and said, "I see you're expecting, my dear. When are you due?"

"The first week in April," Susan answered.

"And your husband? Where is he?"

The words hung in the air like a trapeze artist suspended between the swing and the catcher. Everyone looked at Susan. She looked across the table at Armando. His mouth was drawn into a tight, straight line. She knew he wanted her to say, as he had, that her husband had been killed in an accident. Instead she said, "I'm not married."

"Oh?" The woman who had asked the question blushed. "I'm sorry," she said. "I didn't mean...I shouldn't have asked."

"That's all right. I understand." Susan smiled. "The music is wonderful, isn't it? I love mariachis. We hear them in Texas occasionally."

And one of the brothers said, "Oh, you're from Texas," and he began, rather nervously, to talk about Texas.

Dammit, Armando thought, why hadn't Susan lied? What would it have cost her to say, 'My husband is dead?' It wasn't anybody's business about the baby. Now everyone was curious. They darted surreptitious glances his way, as though to ask how it was that he and this young American woman had become friends.

A little before seven Inocencia and Francisco told everyone goodbye so that they could catch the evening train to Mexico City. From there they were going to fly to Mazatlan for a two-week honeymoon.

Armando and Susan drove them to the train station. Inocencia hugged Susan and said, "I'm going to miss you."

"And I'll miss you. Have a wonderful time. I'll see you when you get back." She kissed Francisco's cheek and said, "Happy honeymoon."

Then the newlyweds boarded and when they had found their seats, they waved.

"They look so happy," Susan said. "And I'm so happy for them."

"Yes, so am I." But Armando didn't look happy.

When they returned to the ranch, the party was still going on. The mariachis continued to play and some of the guests were dancing. But Susan, after a dance with one of Inocencia's brothers, went to sit beside Sophia.

"You're tired, aren't you?" Sophia asked.

"Yes," Susan admitted. "It's been a long day."

"Do you feel all right?"

Susan nodded. "Except for my back. It hurts."

"That will get worse."

"Thanks a lot," Susan said with a laugh.

"How are you and Armando getting along?" Sophia peered at her through the darkness. "Is the baby his?"

Susan stared at the elderly woman in surprise. "No, no, of course not. I was two and a half months pregnant when I met Armando."

"Where is the father?"

"In Houston."

"You have no intention of marrying him?"

"No."

"What about Armando?"

"What do you mean?"

"Are you going to marry him? Has he asked you to?"

Susan hesitated. She really didn't want to discuss this with Sophia. She knew that Armando was angry with her for having told the truth about her pregnancy and she wanted to drop the whole thing. But Sophia wasn't to be put off.

"Well?" she asked with a thump of her cane. "Well?"

"Yes," Susan said. "Armando has asked me to marry him. But—"

"But you refused?" Sophia leaned closer. With her chin thrust forward she said, "Good Lord! Why did you do that?"

"I wanted to wait until after the baby comes."

"But why?"

"I thought it best, Sophia. Best for Armando, I mean."

"I see." The old lady remained silent for a few moments. "You love him, don't you?"

"Yes, I love him." Susan looked out to where Armando stood talking to the judge. He had one foot up on the fountain, a glass of champagne in his hand. In his gray flannel pants and dark blue cashmere jacket he looked as handsome as she'd ever seen him. She had watched him today during the ceremony and for a moment she had wished that it had been she and Armando who were being married. Silently she had repeated the vows that Inocencia and Francisco had taken. Silently she had repeated, I, Susan, take thee Armando...

"Don't wait," Sophia said, breaking in on her thoughts. "Marry him now before he changes his mind. Give your child a name, let him be a Cobian. If you marry after the baby's born, Armando will have no legal obligation to give the child his name."

"But I thought..." Susan stopped herself. No, she hadn't thought. She had assumed that when they were married her child would have Armando's name. But what if Armando didn't want that? What if he said, Give him your name or his father's name, he isn't mine? Could she live with that? Could she continue to love him if he said that?

When the hour grew late and Sophia had nodded off in her chair, Susan told the other guests good-night. But instead of going to bed, she decided to take a walk.

The night had grown cold and she pulled the dark blue poncho close around her shoulders. As she moved farther away from the house she could hear the music of the mariachis. The sound of crickets played a bass accompaniment and somewhere in the distance a dog barked.

The smell of winter hung in the air, as cold and crisp as hoarfrost. She looked up at the clear night sky and breathed deeply. January, February and March. Then it would be April and her baby would come. She put her hands over her stomach. "I love you," she said. "I love you, baby mine."

She leaned on the corral fence and thought what it would be like to hold her child in her arms. She wondered if it would be a boy or a girl, and she began turning names over in her head. Her father's name had been Stanley, and although she had loved her father and there was nothing wrong with the name Stanley, she didn't think she wanted to name her son that. If she had a son. She was just as doubtful about girl's names. "Wait until the little critter is born before you decide what to name him," Maria had advised in a recent letter, and that's what Susan had decided to do.

When she began to shiver with the cold, she went to the stable. The foal that had been born when she first came to the ranch was a colt now. Long and lean, with wonderful lines and straight legs, he was as gangly as an adolescent, with back legs that hadn't quite caught up with his front legs.

He nickered when Susan came down to his stall and when she had fed him a few pieces of sugar, she rubbed the white streak on his forehead and said, "Hello, boy. You're getting to be a real beauty, aren't you?"

He nuzzled her hand, trying to find more sugar and Susan said, "Sorry, Raja. There isn't any more. I'll bring you some tomorrow..." She heard the stable door open and when she looked around, she saw Armando.

"I wondered where you were," he said.

"Has everybody gone?"

He nodded. "I checked the bedroom. When you weren't there I started looking for you. I thought you were tired."

"I was, but I wanted a walk." She scratched the colt's forehead. "Raja's going to be a beauty, isn't he?"

"Yes, he is."

She didn't look at him. "You're angry with me, aren't you?" she said.

Armando hesitated. "I don't see any reason why you found it necessary to announce that you weren't married."

"I didn't *announce* it," Susan said reasonably. "Manuel's wife asked if I was married and I told her the truth."

"Damn it all, Susana, there's no need to tell everybody that you aren't married."

"I prefer that to lying."

His face flushed. "I told Cesar that your husband had been killed in an accident because if I hadn't, he would have assumed the baby was mine."

Susan turned away from him and started out of the stable. But Armando stopped her with a detaining hand on her arm. "That's one solution," he said. "I could tell everyone the child is mine."

Susan stared up at him. "You'd do that?"

"We needn't wait to get married. We could do what Inocencia and Francisco did, just have a civil wedding. There'd be no talk then, everyone knows a first child can come anytime."

Why did she doubt him? Was it because there was something in the tone of his voice, something in his face, that belied his words. It was as though he had told himself this was the correct thing to do and he was trying to do it.

Susan shook her head. "It's decent of you to ask me, Armando, but we've agreed to wait until after the baby is born. I think we should stick to that." She pulled the poncho closer. "I'm cold," she said, and turned away. "I want to go back to the house."

Armando gripped her upper arms. "I love you," he said.

"I know." She touched the side of his face. "I know."

He drew her into his arms. Her face was cool against his and a feeling of helplessness made him tighten his arms around her. It was all so damn complicated. Why couldn't he have met her under different circumstances? If she hadn't been pregnant, if they had just met and fallen in love, everything would have been so easy.

He kissed her, his mouth hard against hers as though to block out all the reasons why loving her wasn't easy. He slid his hands under the poncho and found her breasts and when he did, he groaned into her mouth.

Suddenly, whether from need or the fear that in spite of everything Susan might never be his, Armando's body tightened with desire. The kiss deepened. He ravished her mouth, relishing the sweet taste of her, and when she began to answer his kiss with a fervor that matched his, he knew that he couldn't wait. He had to have her now.

He reached around the back of her dress and began fumbling with her zipper, and when he found it, he pulled it down and the pink dress loosened over her shoulders.

Her breasts filled the pink satin bra. He ran cold fingers over the spilling fullness and she shivered. "I want you," he said, and before she could protest he took her hand and led her into the empty stall next to Raja's.

"We can't..." she started to say.

But Armando was past hearing. He pulled the poncho from her shoulders and spread it down upon the straw. He kissed her again, and when her breath grew hot and her lips trembled against his, he knelt with her on the straw and with frantic hands he began to fondle her breasts.

Susan tried to protest, but when he touched her, the protest died on her lips. She caught fire and began to struggle with the buttons on his shirt so that she could touch him. He took his jacket off, then brought her down beside him on the sweet-smelling straw.

She gave no thought to the new pink dress now. All that mattered was Armando's touch, his closeness. He kissed her breasts and she moaned aloud with pleasure and held herself up to him, an offering to his hungry mouth.

He nuzzled against her, reveling in the sweet fullness of the peaked and swollen nipples. His body grew so taut with desire that he knew he couldn't wait.

Quickly he cast his shoes aside, then his trousers, and raised her dress up over her hips.

They came together with a fierceness that whooshed the breath out of Susan's body. But that didn't matter, nothing mattered except the frantic motion of Armando's body over hers.

"Love you," he whispered. "Need you." He took her mouth. "*Mi preciosa, mi querida* Susana."

Caught in a vortex of passion, she followed where Armando led, every nerve thrumming with desire as she raised her body to his, meeting him thrust for thrust in those final ecstatic moments. In a fever of passion she cried his name, clinging and close as her body spun out of control. She held nothing back; she was totally his, giving everything she had. And when he said, "Yes, oh yes," she took his cry and held him, and it all began again, that wondrous spinning out of control, that bright tumultuous feeling that is unlike any other on this earth.

They lay side by side in the hay while their heartbeats slowed and steadied, listening to the gentle nickering of the horses.

"The English have a saying," Susan murmured, "that almost everything is acceptable as long as you don't do it outside and scare the horses." She kissed his shoulder. "I hope we haven't scared the horses."

Armando chuckled. "I love you," he said as he drew her close within the circle of his arms. "I love you because you make me laugh and because you make me feel so damn good. I look at you or I touch you and I want you so much I can hardly control myself." He kissed the top of her head. "What is it that you do to me, little gringa? What magic do you use to make me feel the way I do?"

"The magic of love," she said.

They stayed like that, with her head on his shoulder and his arms around her. When the stable grew cold they dressed and arm in arm, they went back to the house.

The next morning Armando took Susan back to San Miguelito.

"I have to go to Morelia for a couple of days," he said when he left her. "But I'll be back on Friday and we'll go out to dinner."

"You'll be tired," Susan said. "Why don't I fix dinner here? We can sit in front of the fire and you can just relax."

"If I'm too relaxed I won't be able to drive home."

"That's what I'm hoping," she said against his lips.

On Thursday morning Susan went out to the patio to cut poinsettias for a centerpiece. While Smooch stalked birds that he would never catch, she began to carefully cut the stems of the bright red leaves and place them on the work bench where she kept her empty pots and the trowels.

When she heard a car stop outside her gate, she brushed her hands off on the sides of her blue-and-white checked smock and started across the patio to the gate, sure that it was Armando and pleased that he'd returned a day early.

But when the gate opened the greeting died on her lips.

Zachary Owens, a familiar sardonic smile on his lips, looked around the patio, raised one eyebrow and said, "So this is where you ran off to, Susan. It's rather charming in a rustic bohemian kind of way, isn't it? I can't say much for the neighborhood, though. Cobblestone streets filled with skinny dogs and runny-nosed brats." He flicked at a speck of dust on his tailor-made slacks.

"What . . . ?" Susan grasped at the back of one of the patio chairs. "What are you doing here?"

"I came to see you, of course."

"Why?"

"I was curious." His gaze traveled down her body. "I wanted to see if you really were pregnant." He chuckled. "And I see that you are. When's the blessed event, Susan?"

She ran a tongue over her lips. "In April," she said.

"I presume you're going back to Houston to have the baby."

"No." She let go of the chair and took a step backward. "Why have you come?" she asked.

"I came to see you." Zachary sat down and stretched his legs out in front of him. "Surely you don't plan to have our baby in this godforsaken place."

"*Our* baby?" Susan started to tremble. "It's my baby, Zachary. It has nothing to do with you."

"Have you forgotten that I'm its father, dear?" He reached in a side pocket and took out his pipe, tapped it, then reached in his back pocket for a pouch of tobacco, filled the pipe, then lit it with a gold lighter. With a smile that sent a chill through her body he said, "I'm afraid I overreacted that day in my office. I tried to talk to you later, but you refused to see me. I've thought about you often these last few months, Susan, and when I found out where you were—"

"How did you find out?"

"I went to Granbury. Your family's neighbor, old Mr. Norman, told me you were in Mexico. He said some mail had come to the house and your mailman had told him you were in a place called San Miguelito." He smoothed one manicured finger across his neatly trimmed moustache. "Really, Susan, this doesn't suit you at all. You don't belong here, you belong back in Houston."

He got up and started toward her. "That's why I've come. I'm going to take you back with me."

Her face went pale. "You're what?"

"I'm going to take you back to Houston with me. I have a beach house in Galveston. You and the baby can live there." Before Susan could step away he reached out and took her hands. "If things work out between us we can talk about marriage. I'm forty-two. Perhaps it's time I settled down."

Susan yanked her hands away. She couldn't believe that even Zachary could be this presumptuous. He had raped her, thrown money at her, and now he expected

her to forget everything and come docilely back to
Houston with him.

"I know I behaved badly that day in the office," he
said. "But I've had women try that pregnancy routine
on me before. How was I to know that you really were
pregnant?"

"Forget that day in the office, Zachary! What about
the night you raped me?"

"Raped you?" Zachary laughed and shook his head.
"Come on, Susan, it was hardly rape. We'd been dating for months. You knew I cared for you." He took a
step toward her. "I admit that I had too much to drink
that night and that perhaps I got a bit too amorous. But
you looked so delicious that I—"

"Too amorous!" She wanted to hit him. She wanted
to smash that supercilious look off his too-handsome-
face and send him howling out her gate and out of her
life.

"Don't exaggerate, Susan. We both know you wanted
it just as much as I did that night."

"Get out of here!" She clenched her hands to her
sides to keep from striking out at him. "Just get the hell
out of here, Zachary."

He shook his head. "I'd hoped you'd invite me for
lunch so that we could have a little chat." He smiled,
showing his perfect white teeth. "You make a very
beautiful pregnant lady," he said. "I've thought a lot
about you since you've been gone. I think perhaps I was
a fool to let you go, particularly when you're carrying
our child."

"It's my child," she said again.

But Zachary only shook his head and smiled, kindly,
patiently. "It's mine, as well, dear girl. Never forget
that. Take a day or two to think about what I've said,

Susan. I could make life quite comfortable for you and the child, you know. I'd see you almost every weekend. You'd just have to be there for me when I wanted you."

"Get out!" Close to hysteria now, trembling with rage, Susan started toward him.

He laughed and in mock fear held his hands in front of him as though protecting himself. "I'll be back," he said, and still laughing he went out and closed the gate behind him.

Susan waited until she heard the car start. Then, with a sob, she turned and ran into the house. She barely made it into the bathroom before she was ill.

Finally, pale and shaking with reaction, she stumbled into the bedroom and lay across the bed.

Zachary was here. My God! What was she going to do?

All of her instincts told her to run. What if Zachary wanted the child? He was an attorney, a partner in one of the most important law offices in Houston. What if he took her to court and demanded custody?

She put her hands protectively over her stomach. He wouldn't do that. He couldn't.

But what if he could?

She began to cry then, great wrenching sobs that shook her body and hurt her throat. God, how she hated him. How she'd like to smash that suave smile off his face.

But that wouldn't do any good. Nor would running away solve the problem. She had to face Zachary, she had to show him she wasn't afraid.

If only Armando were here.... Armando! What would he do when he found out that Zachary was in San Miguelito? Would he blame her? Would he think that

Zachary had come because he cared about her? Would he think she had lied about the rape?

Susan curled herself into a fetal position, her arms across her belly as though to shield her child. And she wept, hot bitter tears, for what had happened and for fear of what would happen.

Armando called from Morelia that night. "How are you?" he asked. "Is everything all right?"

Susan tightened her hand around the phone. "Everything's fine," she said.

"You sure? You sound a little strange."

"Maybe I'm getting a cold." She hesitated, then said, "Armando?"

"Yes, dear? What is it?"

She took a deep breath. "Nothing. I—I miss you, that's all."

"And I miss you, Susan. I wish I were there, *querida*. I wish I could hold you and go to sleep with you."

"Tomorrow," she said, and wondered why she had started to cry again.

"Yes, tomorrow. Good night, little love."

"Good night, Armando."

Susan put the phone down. "You should have told him," she said aloud. She reached for the phone again, half tempted to call him back. Then she shook her head.

I'll tell him tomorrow, she thought.

And prayed that Zachary would stay away.

Chapter Twelve

Susan didn't go to her Spanish class that day because the thought of meeting Zachary on the streets of San Miguelito terrified her. She knew she'd have to face him again, but she needed time before she did.

"If anyone except Señor Cobian comes, tell them I'm not in," she instructed Esperanza. And when the woman raised questioning eyebrows, Susan said, "I'm not feeling well. I don't want to be disturbed."

When Esperanza left at two-thirty, Susan locked the door and closed the drapes. At five o'clock she bathed and dressed in black velvet pants and a loose-fitting turquoise top.

She put candles on the pink linen tablecloth and set the table. At six she put the chicken in and began to prepare scalloped potatoes. When that was in the oven, she boiled the artichokes and prepared the salad.

And every time she heard a car her stomach tightened with alarm.

It was almost seven before Armando arrived. When Susan heard the gate open she peeked out from behind the drapes and sighed with relief when she saw Armando striding toward her across the patio.

With a glad cry she opened the door and almost flew into his arms.

"What a reception," he said with a laugh. "I'll have to go away more often."

Between laughter and tears, Susan hugged him and hid her face against his shoulder, so glad to see him she could barely speak.

"Hey," he said, holding her away from him. "What's the matter? Haven't you been feeling well?"

Susan shook her head and rubbed her tears away against his tweed jacket. "I—I guess I've just had the blues."

She knew she had to tell him about Zachary and she promised herself she would. After dinner. When they were relaxing in front of the fire. She'd tell him then.

He gave her the two dozen red roses he'd dropped onto a chair when she rushed into his arms and went out to the kitchen with her while she arranged them in a vase.

"They're beautiful." Susan smiled at him. "And I love you."

He carried the roses in and put them in the center of the pink tablecloth. "Is dinner ready or can we sit down for a few minutes?"

"There's plenty of time. Would you like a glass of wine?"

And when he said he would, she poured it for him and they sat together on the sofa in front of the fireplace.

Armando put his arms around her and pulled her close. "I've missed you," he said against her hair. "I hate being away from you, especially when Inocencia isn't here." He looked down at her. "You sure you're feeling all right?"

"Yes, I'm sure."

Tell him, a voice inside Susan's head warned. She took a deep breath. "Armando, I—"

"It was a great trip," he said. "I've arranged for the purchase of an Arabian stallion. It'll be shipped from Spain sometime next month." He took a tissue-wrapped package out of his pocket and handed it to her. "I bought these for you in Morelia," he said. And when she opened the package she saw a string of colorful wooden beads.

"The Tarascan Indians make them," he told Susan. "I thought you might like them."

"I love them, Armando. Thank you." She put the necklace on over her head, then raised her face for his kiss. And, oh, it was wonderful to be held by him again. He kissed her and his lips were so warm and sweet against hers that for a moment she forgot about Zachary.

The kiss deepened. He began to caress her breasts through the fabric of the blouse, but when she sighed with pleasure and moved closer, he held her away from him. With a chuckle he said, "I love you and I'd like nothing better than to carry you into the bedroom right now and make love to you. But I haven't eaten since breakfast and if you don't feed me soon I'm going to take a bite out of you." He kissed her nose. "Okay?"

"Okay." Susan made a face. "You can light the candles while I get things ready."

She was smiling when she went into the kitchen. Armando put a Ravel tape on the stereo and she could hear him humming along with it. It's going to be all right, she told herself. We'll have dinner and afterward I'll tell him about Zachary.

Someone knocked at the door. Her heart began beating hard against her ribs and she clutched the edge of the sink for support.

She heard Zachary's voice, then Armando's. Armando called out, "There's someone here to see you, Susana."

Dear God, she thought. Dear God.

Hands clenched tight to her sides, Susan went into the living room. "What are you doing here?" she asked Zachary.

He raised one arrogant eyebrow. "Aren't you going to introduce me to your friend?"

Susan's mouth tightened. She looked at Armando, saw the questioning look in his eyes and took a deep breath.

"Armando..." She took another step into the room. "Armando, this is Zachary Owens."

"Zachary...?" Armando's jaw hardened.

"I see Susan has told you about me," Zachary said with a laugh. "An exaggerated version of our brief but lovely affair, I imagine. But then our Susan often exaggerates."

"What are you doing here?" Armando advanced a step.

"I've come to see my girl," Zachary said.

For a moment there was only silence. Armando looked at Susan. "Did you know he was in San Miguelito?"

"He—he came yesterday morning."

"Here? To the house?"

Before she could answer, Zachary said, "I came hoping Susan would invite me for lunch. The food at the hotel is unbelievably bad and a wine list is non-existent." He turned to Susan. "I can't imagine you in a place like this. It's not your style at all." He looked at Armando. "I've come to take her back to Houston," he said. And before Susan could stop him he reached out and patted her stomach. "Susan and little Zach."

"Get your hands off her," Armando snarled.

Zachary's eyes widened in pretended surprise. He grinned at Susan. "So that's how it is. Found yourself a macho Mexican, have you?" He lifted the wooden beads that hung between her breasts. "I can't say I admire his taste in jewelry." He shook his head. "Really, dear, I didn't think wetbacks were your style. You—"

Susan hit him, hard across his face. "Get out!" she cried.

Zachary's fingers were still curled around the necklace, and when he stepped back the string broke and the beads clattered against the tile floor.

Susan advanced. She shoved him, one hand flat against his chest. "You...bastard!" Both words were punctuated by another push. "Get out of here. Out of my life."

Zachary's face, except for the red hand print where she had slapped him, had gone as white as hers. "How dare you?" he said. "You ignorant little slut—"

Armando grabbed Zachary's arm, twisted it up behind him and propelled him out the door.

"Wait!" Susan cried. "Armando, don't!"

But Armando didn't hear. The blood pounded against his ears. He shoved the other man out into the patio and as soon as Zachary turned around, Armando hit him.

Zachary staggered back, one hand to his face. "You broke my nose!" he screamed. He rushed Armando, barreled into him, fists flying. But before he could land a punch, Armando hit him again. Zachary grunted, but he didn't back away. He struck Armando a glancing blow on the side of his face. Armando countered with a right to the jaw and Zachary fell to one knee.

"Get up!" Armando growled. "Get up, you sorry son of a bitch."

Zachary started to push up. When his hand touched a flower pot, he grabbed it and came up swinging. Armando tried to duck, but the heavy pot caught him on one side of his head and smashed him backward.

He heard Susan scream. He saw Zachary lift the pot again and he rolled to one side. The pot crashed inches from his head. He jumped up and rushed the other man.

Zachary backed away. He stumbled against Susan's work bench, reached behind him and grabbed a sharp-edged trowel.

"Mexican bastard!" he cried as he lunged at Armando, arm raised above his head, waiting for an opportunity to strike.

Armando feinted one way, then the other. Zachary danced back and Armando lunged for his wrist, caught it and twisted. The trowel clattered against the tile. Armando took a half step back and with all his weight behind it, he shot a short stiff punch to Zachary's face.

Zachary slammed backward, staggered across the patio and fell. He tried to get up, but before he could, Armando was on him.

Armando struck Zachary in the face, hard punishing blows, swearing Spanish obscenities he hadn't used since he'd been a smart-aleck teenager. Blood ran down his face from the wound on his head, but it didn't matter.

Nothing mattered but punishing this man. He wanted to kill him. He was going to kill him. He didn't deserve to live. He—

"Stop it!" Susan grabbed his shoulders. "Stop it!" she cried. "You're going to kill him."

"I want to kill him." Armando struck Zachary again. "*¡Cabron!*" he panted. "Sorry, rotten, stinking *pendejo!*"

"Armando, stop it!" Hands fastened in his jacket, Susan tried to yank him back. "Stop it," she screamed.

He swung around. "Get in the house!" he thundered.

"Don't hit him again."

Armando struggled to his feet. Hands still curled into fists, he took a step toward her. "Dammit, I told you to get in the house!"

Susan looked at him, her eyes wide with shock, then without a word she turned and ran into the house.

Armando bent over Zachary and pulled him to his feet. Zachary staggered. His head bounced against his chest. Armando led him over to the work bench. He picked up a bucket and propping the other man against the bench, he filled the bucket with water and poured it over Zachary's head.

Zachary snorted, then he moaned and whispered, "I'm hurt."

"Not as hurt as you're going to be if you don't get out of San Miguelito." He steered Zachary toward the gate. "Do you have a car?"

Zachary nodded.

"Can you see?"

Zachary looked up at him. His eyes were swollen. "Think so," he mumbled.

Armando half walked, half carried him out to his car. He opened the door, then he went through Zachary's pockets until he found the keys. "Go back to your hotel and pack your bags," he said. "There's an eight o'clock bus in the morning that will get you to Texas in twelve hours. Be on it."

"I'm going to get the police." Zachary slurred the words. "Going to have you arrested for—"

Armando shoved him hard against the side of the car. "Listen to me," he said. "In Mexico when one of our women has been raped we don't go to the police. We take care of it ourselves." He tightened his hand on the front of Zachary's shirt. "You get on that bus in the morning or you're a dead man."

Zachary stared at him. "Awright," he muttered. "Keep her if you want her. I sure as hell don't, not after she's been sleeping with you. You're welcome to her and to the kid, too. I don't want the little bastard." He looked up at Armando and something like a smile cracked his bruised and bloodied lips. "You going to enjoy raising my kid, Mexican? What if he looks like me? How are you going to like looking at him every day and knowing I had her first?"

"Shut up!"

"Sure." Zachary laughed then winced. "Sure," he said again, and crawled into the car.

It took him a moment to find the ignition and when he did, he started the car. Then he raised his hand in a mock salute and gunning the engine, he went off down the hill.

Armando leaned against the gate. Breathing hard, he tried to suck air into his lungs. He flexed his right hand and saw his torn and bleeding knuckles. Never before had he wanted to kill a man, but he'd wanted to kill

Zachary Owens. He would have if Susana hadn't stopped him.

Armando turned and saw her standing in the doorway. He remembered then that he had shouted at her, and suddenly a feeling of despair gripped him. He leaned his head against the iron gate and closed his eyes. Then he turned and went back to her.

Susan bathed his face. She wiped away the blood, murmuring all the while, "Oh my God. My God." She touched the cut on the side of his head where Zachary had hit him with the pot. "You should see a doctor," she said. "This should have stitches."

Armando shook his head. "Just put a bandage over it. Have you got a couple of aspirin?"

"Yes, of course." Susan opened the bathroom cabinet, took out two aspirin and handed him a glass of water. He drank it down and nodded his thanks.

She lifted his right hand. "Your poor hand," she said, and there were tears in her eyes. She ran cold water in the basin and began to bathe it.

Armando winced when the water touched his bloody knuckles. "Why didn't you tell me he was here in San Miguelito?"

"I was going to."

"Were you?" He looked at her.

"Of course."

"When? After he'd left town? Or had you thought you might decide to go back to Houston with him?"

"How can you even ask that?"

Armando shrugged. "When was he here?"

"Yesterday morning. I was going to tell you right after dinner." She patted his hand dry with a towel. "I wanted to tell you last night when you called but I was too upset." Susan hesitated. "Zachary's an attorney in a prominent law firm. He's an influential man in Houston politics...." She looked at Armando, then away. "I was afraid he'd try to take the baby."

Armando shook his head. "You don't need to worry about that." He shoved the towel away. "I'm tired," he said. "I'd better get going."

"But I thought..." Susan tightened her hands on the towel. "I thought you were going to stay here tonight."

"No, I—I'd better not." He didn't look at her. "I've got things to do on the ranch in the morning. I'd better get home."

"I'm sorry."

"Don't say that again," he said more sharply than he had intended. "This isn't your fault."

"Isn't it?" Susan wanted to throw herself into his arms and beg him to stay. She needed him tonight, needed him to hold her and tell her that Zachary didn't matter, that he loved her and nothing that had happened would ever change that.

But his face looked so closed, and it seemed to her that he held himself away, as though he had already left her.

When they walked out of the bathroom, Armando picked up his jacket.

"The dinner's still warm," Susan said carefully. "Why don't you have something to eat before you go?"

"No thanks, I'm not hungry." A few of the wooden beads rolled against his shoe. He bent down, picked them up, looked at them for a moment, then went over and tossed them into the fireplace. "They weren't any good anyway," he said.

"I'm sorry the evening turned out this way, but I..." He struggled to get the words out. "I have to be alone tonight."

Susan dug her nails into her palms so that she wouldn't cry in front of him. "I'm so sorry," she said again.

"I'll call you tomorrow."

She nodded and waited for him to kiss her.

But he didn't. He hesitated for a moment, then he turned and hurried out the door.

Susan watched him cross the patio. When he reached the gate he opened it, then closed it from the other side. She waited for him to turn back. But he didn't.

She heard the pickup drive away and still she stood, there in the doorway, waiting, hoping that Armando would come back to her.

The street outside grew quiet. At last she went in and closed the door.

She knelt on the floor and began to pick up the wooden beads. It was then that she began to cry.

In the beam of his headlights it seemed to Armando as though he could still see Zachary Owens's face, the sardonic smile, the raised eyebrow. And in the whirr of the tires against the black macadam he could hear Owens's voice. *What if he looks like me? How will you like looking at him every day and knowing I had her first?*

Armando slammed his fist against the steering wheel and his hand started to bleed again. He reached in his pocket, took out his handkerchief and, using his teeth, managed to wrap it around his hand.

Never before had he wanted to wound another human being, but he had wanted to wound the man who had raped Susana, he'd wanted to kill him.

He wasn't sure why he had left her tonight, he'd only known that he had to get away, that it would have been impossible for him to have lain in the same bed with her.

Armando thought of the baby she carried in her womb, Zachary Owens's baby, and the bitterness of bile rose like poison in his throat. God help him, he knew now that he could never accept the child, not after he'd met the father, not after he'd seen what kind of a bastard he was.

In his mind's eye he pictured Zachary Owens. He saw again that sardonically superior smile, the neatly clipped moustache, the tailor-made suit and the white silk shirt. Armando struck the steering wheel again and sucked in his breath at the pain. "Damn him to hell," Armando said aloud. "Damn him to blazing, eternal hell."

How could Susana even have dated a man like that? Hadn't she been able to see through the suave phoniness? How could she have let a man like that kiss her, touch her...?

Sickness rose again. Armando clenched his teeth and swallowed hard. Owens had made love to her—no, not love, he had had sex with her. He had been inside her, he...

Tears stung Armando's eyes. Don't think like that, he told himself. Nothing that has happened has been Susan's fault. She couldn't help it.

But if she hadn't been dating him this wouldn't have happened, a voice inside his head whispered. What had she worn the night she had gone out with Zachary? Had the dress been too tight, cut too low? Why had she allowed Zachary to come into her apartment? Had she deliberately led him on or had she thought she could handle him if he got too amorous. Had they kissed and touched each other, the way he and Susan touched?

Had she tried hard enough to get away from him? Couldn't she have done something? Couldn't she have screamed louder? Fought harder?

Why hadn't she gone to the police that night? Why had she remained silent?

So preoccupied was he with his thoughts that he almost missed the turnoff to his ranch. But when at last he was there, he stopped the car and leaned his head against the steering wheel. Susana. He loved her, but he knew, deep down in the recesses of his heart, that he could never accept the child she carried.

When Armando went in, he stripped off his torn and bloody clothes and stood under a stinging hot shower. The phone was ringing when he came out with a towel wrapped around his waist. He picked it up and Susan said, "Armando? I just wanted to make sure you got home safely." He heard the hesitancy in her voice. "To make sure that you're all right."

"I'm okay," he said. "I just got out of the shower."

"I'm so sorry about what happened."

He tightened his hand around the phone. "It wasn't your fault."

"Will I see you tomorrow?"

"I don't think so. There are things I have to do around the ranch."

"Then you'll be busy for a while."

"Yes, for a while."

"I see."

"I'll call you."

For a moment Susan didn't answer. Then she said, "Good night, Armando."

The receiver clicked. Armando stood for a moment with his hand on the phone. There was a part of him that wanted to call her back, that wanted to get in his car and drive back to San Miguelito.

He took a deep breath, then he went over to his bed. He sat on the edge of it, his head in his hands. "What am I going to do?" he whispered. "What in the name of all that's holy am I going to do?"

Chapter Thirteen

Be careful!" Susan frowned up at Esperanza who stood on a step stool reaching up into the cupboard. "I'm taller than you are. I know where the tuna is, let me get it."

"You are *embarazada*. You should not be on a ladder." Esperanza rose on her tiptoes and stretched out her arm. Suddenly the stool skidded away from her. She cried out, flailing her arms in the air, and Susan, without conscious thought, reached out to break her fall. Both women fell, Esperanza on top of Susan.

Esperanza pushed herself away from Susan, screaming, "*¡Ay, Dios mio!* What have I done? Have I hurt you? I'm sorry. *Ay, Dios*, I'm so sorry."

Susan took a deep breath. Momentarily stunned, afraid to move, she managed to say, "I—I'm all right. What about you?"

Esperanza started to cry. "Let me help you up." She knelt beside Susan and put an arm around Susan's shoulders.

"No, wait. I'd better lie here for a minute."

"I'll call the doctor."

"No, I'm all right, Esperanza. I don't think we have to call Dr. Garcia."

"Then I'll call Señor Cobian."

Susan shook her head. "No, don't call him." She raised herself into a sitting position, then reached out for Esperanza to help her up. For a moment she clung to the other woman. She felt a little dizzy, slightly nauseous. With her hands protectively over her stomach she said, "Maybe you're right Esperanza. Maybe we'd better call Dr. Garcia."

Esperanza put her arm around Susan's waist to help her into the living room. "How many months do you have?" she asked in a worried voice.

"A little over six."

Esperanza drew her breath in. She put her hand over Susan's stomach. "Do you have any pain?"

"No." She looked at Esperanza, concern putting an edge to her voice. "You've had ten children," she said. "Did you ever fall or hurt yourself? Did . . ." She heard the gate squeak open, then Inocencia's voice calling out, "Susana? Are you there?"

"Gracias a Dios," Esperanza cried. "It is Señora Inocencia." She ran to the door and called out, "Come quickly. There has been an accident."

Inocencia, with Francisco only a few steps behind her, ran across the patio to the house.

"What happened?" she cried, and before Susan could answer, Esperanza, with much weeping and wringing of her hands, began rattling off Spanish too rapid for Susan to understand.

"I'm okay," Susan said. "How was your honeymoon? Did you like Mazatlan? How..." She grabbed Inocencia's arm. "I'm dizzy," she said.

Francisco put his arm around her and led her to the sofa. And Inocencia said, "Call the hospital, Francisco. Tell Dr. Garcia we're taking her there."

"Do you really think I have to? Maybe if I just went to bed—"

"It's best to see the doctor, Susana." Francisco patted her hand. "He'll want to have a look at you."

He dialed, spoke into the phone and when he replaced it he said, "Garcia's at the hospital. He'll meet us there."

"This is a fine welcome home for you," Susan grumbled when Esperanza went to get her coat. "I wasn't sure when you were due back, but I wanted to do something special when you returned, dinner...something."

"You can do it later," Inocencia said. "Right now we're going to get you to the hospital."

"But I feel perfectly all right. I..." Susan gasped and her face twisted with pain.

"What is it?" Inocencia grasped her arm.

"Pains. Here." Susan put her hands over the lower part of her stomach.

Inocencia and Francisco exchanged looks. Then Francisco scooped Susan up in his arms. "Take her coat," he told Inocencia when Esperanza ran in with it.

"What's happening?" Esperanza asked, her eyes wide with apprehension.

"Susana's having some pain," Inocencia said. "Open the door, will you? Dr. Garcia's waiting for us at the hospital."

"So much fuss," Susan said, and tried to smile.

But she was more afraid than she'd ever been in her life, afraid that something was happening to her baby.

Francisco hurried across the patio to the gate. The pain came again, hard, contracting, hurting, but she tried not to show it when he put her in the car.

He drove as carefully as he could down the cobblestone street to town, but with each jolt Susan felt a stab of pain from her stomach to her back. Please, she silently prayed. Oh, please don't let anything happen to my baby.

Dr. Garcia, a short man with a hard square body and kind brown eyes, met them at the hospital entrance. He nodded a brief hello to Francisco and Inocencia and turned his attention to Susan.

"*¿Que le pasa?*" he asked when she was wheeled into the emergency room on a gurney. "What is all this business about a fall?"

"Not much of a fall. Esperanza, my maid, fell and when I tried to catch her she landed on top of me." Susan put her hand on his arm. "I'm not going to lose the baby, am I? Please don't let that happen. Please, I—"

"*Calma*, Señorita Susana. Don't worry." He motioned to the nurse and the orderly, and together they put Susan up on the examining table.

The nurse stayed with her and held her hand while Dr. Garcia examined her. She had another pain, this one sharper than the others.

A frown creased the doctor's forehead. "How bad is it?" he asked.

Susan saw the look. "Not—not too bad. What does it mean? Am I miscarrying? What's happening?"

"I'm not sure yet, Susana. Try to lie still now."

He finished his examination. "I think you're going to be all right," he said at last, "but I want to keep you here today and tonight for observation. Now let's see if you have any injuries." He touched a scratch on her cheek and said something to the nurse before he began running his hands down Susan's body. He checked her legs, then her arms, and when he touched her left ankle she said, "Ow, wow, that hurts."

"It's a sprain," Garcia said. "We'll take care of it. We're going to take you to a room now and I want you to rest. Try not to worry. The chances are very good that the baby is all right."

The chances? Susan put her hands over her stomach. Oh, please, she silently prayed, please don't let anything happen to my baby.

When she was in bed, Inocencia came in. "I sent Francisco home," she told Susan. "I'll stay with you."

"You don't have to. I'll be all right."

"But I'd rather be here." She patted Susan's hand. "The doctor said you should rest, so I want you to close your eyes and try to sleep. I'll be right here. Francisco is going to call Armando."

"No, I don't want him to know about this."

"But he would want to know, Susana." Inocencia moved a chair close to Susan's bed. "Try to rest now."

But Susan shook her head. She was too scared to rest. "Tell me about your honeymoon," she said.

"It was lovely. We stayed in a hotel right on the sea, in an oceanfront room. At night we went to sleep with the sound of the waves pounding against the shore." A shy smile curled the corners of her lips. "In all the time Francisco and I have known each other this was the first time we really slept together. It was such joy, Susana, to go to sleep in his arms and to wake up with him beside me. Never in my life have I known such contentment. It's difficult to explain, but it is as if in Francisco I have found the other half of myself. For the first time in my life I feel complete.''

She patted Susan's hand. "But I'm talking too much and you need to rest. Close your eyes, muchacha," she soothed, and began to stroke Susan's arm. "I'll be right here."

But it was a long time before Susan closed her eyes and drifted off... off to a meadow filled with wildflowers and babies. She began to run through the meadow, laughing with pleasure at the turned-up faces that grew along with the flowers. There were chubby babies, delicate babies, brown and black and white babies. She picked one up and tossed it into the air where it floated, light as a feather, until she plucked it from the sky and put it down beside a cluster of wood violets.

But where was her baby? She ran on, looking at all of the little faces, trying to find that one special face among the flowers.

Clouds scudded across a darkening sky and her heart began to pound with fear. Where was her baby? Why couldn't she find her baby? She cried out, "Come back, come back. Oh, please..."

"Susana," Armando said. "Wake up, *querida*. You're dreaming."

She opened her eyes. "Where...?" Still in the throes of her dream, unsure of where she was, she clung to Armando's arm. "I couldn't find my baby," she whispered. "I looked and looked and I couldn't find him."

"It was only a dream." Armando brought her hand to his lips and kissed her fingertips.

"A dream?"

"Yes, Susana."

A sigh shivered through her body. "I had an accident," she said.

"I know. Francisco phoned me." Armando tightened his hand around hers, remembering the terrible stab of fear he'd known when he learned that Susan was in the hospital. He had gone out to look at a new piece of pastureland that had only recently been planted, and when he had ridden in, Juanita had been waiting for him.

"Señor Gutierez telephoned three hours ago," she'd said. "There has been an accident. Señorita Susana is in the hospital."

He had stared at Juanita for a moment, then, without waiting to change his clothes, he'd jumped in his truck and raced toward San Miguelito.

Inocencia had been with Susana. "I came as soon as I heard," he'd said in a low voice. "How is she?"

"She hasn't had any more pains, but it's still too early to tell."

"What in the hell happened?"

"Esperanza was standing on a step stool. She slipped and Susan tried to catch her. Esperanza fell on top of her."

Armando had cursed under his breath. Susana had looked so pale and still lying there in the narrow bed. There were dark patches under her eyes and a scratch on her cheek. Something grabbed at his insides and hot tears stung his eyes. He wanted to gather Susana up in his arms, to hold her close so that he would know she was safe.

"A nurse has been coming in to check on her," Inocencia had whispered. "But she doesn't tell me anything." She lifted her shoulders in a helpless gesture. "I think all we can do now is wait until morning when the doctor sees her.''

"You go home," he'd said. "I'll stay with her. Call Francisco. Have him come for you."

Inocencia had been reluctant to leave, but finally when Armando assured her that he would stay, she left. That had been over an hour ago.

"You didn't have to come," Susan said now.

"Yes, I did." Armando squeezed her hand, then helping her up a bit he gave her some apple juice to drink. "I'm sorry I haven't called you," he said.

Susan looked up at him. A week had gone by since Armando's fight with Zachary, but there were still bruises on his face and a cut over his left eye that hadn't quite healed. The knuckles of his right hand looked pink and tender. But Susan knew it hadn't been only the visible bruises that had hurt Armando. Coming face-to-face with Zachary had been traumatic for him. But it had been traumatic for her, too, and she had wanted to share the way she felt with him. It had hurt her when he hadn't called.

But he was here now, holding her hand to help her through her fear, telling her that everything was going to be all right.

He told her to go back to sleep, and when her eyelids fluttered, he began to stroke her forehead and to whisper, "Go to sleep, Susana. Go to sleep, *querida*. I'm here, I won't leave you."

He knew how desperately she wanted the baby, how hurt she would be if something happened. He loved her so much, but there was a fear mixed with the loving because she was so vulnerable, so fragile. He told himself that women had been having babies for centuries, but this was Susana and if anything happened to her, he wouldn't want to go on because life would have no meaning without her.

He had loved her since that autumn day they'd gone riding in the hills above the ranch. He had kissed her that day and it had been like a coming home; he'd known he had found the woman he'd been searching for all his life.

If there hadn't been any baby, they would have been married now. Perhaps she would be carrying his child. Perhaps... But it was Zachary's child that she carried.

It might have been different if he hadn't met Owens. Perhaps in time he would have come to accept the child. But he *had* met Owens, he'd seen what kind of a man he was, and he knew that he could never accept an off-spring of such a man. He could not live every day of his life with the reminder of the man who had created the child.

Armando sat by Susan's bed all through the long night, tortured by his thoughts, loving Susan, hating his own meanness of spirit, his inability to understand or accept why she wanted to keep the child.

She looked very young and as innocent as he had first thought her to be. Her chestnut hair spread in a cloud of softness against the white pillowcase. One hand lay across her stomach as though even in sleep she was protecting the tiny being who grew there. If something happened to her because of this... if she died...

With a smothered moan, Armando put his arms on the bed and leaned his head close to her hip because he needed to be near her. In a little while he slept, and when he awoke sometime during the night he felt her gently stroking his hair. But he didn't move, he stayed as he was, tears stinging his eyes, overwhelmed by feelings of love. As unobtrusively as he could, he wiped his eyes against the sheet, then raised his head and said, ''What is it, Susana? Are you all right? Do you want anything?''

But her eyes were closed and her breathing was even; the gesture she'd made had been automatic and natural. She'd known he was there and she'd reached out to touch him.

With a sigh, Armando sat up and flexed his shoulders. As quietly as he could he got up and went to stand by the window. Morning was still an hour away, but the darkness of the night had begun to fade. The sky turned to gray with just the faintest tinge of pink, and through the open window he heard the first awakening call of birds and smelled the clean freshness of dew.

He leaned his face against the cool windowpane. He knew now what he was going to do and the thought of it ripped through his gut like a jagged knife. But it was the only way. If Susan agreed, they could go on. If she didn't... He sucked in a great gulp of air. Would she understand how he felt and make the sacrifice because she loved him? He closed his eyes. Yes, Susan loved him. There was a chance she would do as he asked.

Dr. Garcia came in the morning. He asked Armando to leave while he examined Susan.

"There's no spotting," he told her. "I'm pretty sure you're going to be all right. You can go home, but I want you to stay off your feet for at least a week."

And when Susan promised to do exactly that, he patted her shoulder and left.

"I can go home," she told Armando when he came back to her room. "I'll have to rest for a week, but I'm going to be fine." She put her hands over her stomach. "*We're* going to be fine."

"I'm glad," Armando said. He took her hand. "I'll go home with you, Susana, and I'll stay with you until you're well."

She shook her head. "That's not necessary, Armando. Esperanza will be there, and Inocencia will visit."

But he said, "No, Susana. I want to be with you. I want to be the one to take care of you."

There was something in his eyes, an expression that Susan had never seen before, an expression of love and of something else, something that frightened her. She tightened her fingers around his, and because she knew that this was something he needed to do, she said, "All right, Armando. Thank you."

And she tried to quell the shiver of fear that chilled her.

The next few days were quietly pleasant. Every morning Armando, who slept on the sofa, rose early to check on Susan. As soon as she stirred, he went in to make sure she was all right and to ask if he could help her to the bathroom before he went into the kitchen to prepare her breakfast.

While Smooch wound himself in between and around his ankles, he squeezed fresh orange juice, scrambled eggs for an omelet and put milk on to boil for the hot chocolate. Usually by the time breakfast was almost ready, Esperanza had arrived with hot croissants from the bakery. Then, adding a flower from the garden, he would carry the tray in to Susan.

She looked very pretty and fresh on these early mornings, cheerful and relaxed as she chatted with Armando between sips of the chocolate or bites of the omelet.

This time together became more and more important to Armando, for although he and Susan were not sharing a bed, they were sharing a portion of their lives.

It was a very special time for him, and because he knew that it might be the last, the only real time he and Susan would ever have, he cherished it, as he cherished her. He wanted her to be better, but at the same time he wanted these days to go on forever. He loved taking care of her, waiting on her. He loved the way she looked in the morning when her face was rosy from sleep and her long hair curled in disarray over her shoulders. He loved her soft nightgowns, her fastidiousness, her warmth and her humor. He loved everything about her.

As for Susan, because there'd been no more pain or contractions, she was sure now that the baby was all right and that she would carry it full term.

But she didn't speak of the baby to Armando. It was only when Inocencia came in the afternoon so that Armando could check on things at the ranch, that she felt free to say, "The baby's moving, Inocencia. Put your hand here. Feel it?"

And Inocencia would say, "Yes, yes, I feel it. He's kicking. Oh, isn't that incredible, Susana. I can actually feel him."

Sometimes they talked about names. "I can't decide," Susan said. "I've thought of all the boy's names I know and none of them seems right. Maybe I'll know when I look at the baby what his name should be."

"But what if it's a girl? Wouldn't it be nice to have a girl, Susana? Have you thought about girls' names?"

And when Susan said that no, she'd only been thinking about names for boys, Inocencia, barely keeping a straight face, began to suggest the names of long-dead relatives, names like Hortensia, Gertrudis and Begnina, and pretended to look annoyed when Susan giggled.

Each evening when Inocencia and Esperanza had gone, Armando carried Susan into the living room and put her on the sofa in front of the fire. They would eat the dinner that Esperanza had prepared before she left, and sometimes they would watch television on the set that Armando had brought from the ranch. At other times they would talk, but never of the baby or Zachary or of what Susan would do when the baby came.

It was as though they were in limbo, in some strange place where there was no reality, only this space of time where there was no past or future, no need to think of next week or next month or next year.

There were nights when Susan lay alone in her bed that she wanted to call out to him, Armando please come to me. Please hold me and tell me that everything is all right between us.

But she never called, and he never came.

And there were nights when Armando lay on the sofa staring into the dying embers of the fire, nights when he longed to go to Susan, to hold her and tell her how much he loved her and how much she meant to him. But he didn't go. Instead he would put his arm across his eyes to blot out the memory of her face and the sweet softness of her body, her scents and her sighs.

Sometimes he told himself that it was going to be all right. He would tell Susan how he felt and she would understand. They would be married and they'd spend their honeymoon in Paris or Madrid. Yes, he'd take her to Spain. She'd like that. They'd get a place on the Mediterranean where they could spend long, lazy days on the beach. They'd drink sangria and eat paella, and at night they'd listen to the sound of the waves while they made love.

If only she would agree to do what he asked, what needed to be done.

At the end of the week Armando took Susan to the hospital where Dr. Garcia examined her and announced her well and fit.

"You can do almost anything now," he said. "Both you and the baby are fine. He will arrive the first week of April."

"How do you know the baby's a he?" Susan asked with a smile.

"The first child should always be a boy." He winked at Susan. "But you will accept a girl if she comes, yes?"

"Just as long as my baby is healthy," Susan said.

Garcia nodded. "It will be, Señorita Susana. Never fear."

To celebrate the fact that Dr. Garcia had pronounced her well, Armando took Susan to lunch. Because it was a warm and sunny afternoon they sat outside under a striped umbrella. A four-piece mariachi band played at one end of the patio, and waiters in red jackets scurried back and forth with trays of food.

"It feels wonderful to be outside," Susan said. She reached for Armando's hand. "There's no way I can thank you for this week, Armando."

"It wasn't anything, Susana."

"Yes it was," she insisted. "You'll probably be permanently crippled from having slept on the sofa for six days. You won't have to tonight. I mean..." She blushed. "I mean I'm all right now. I asked Dr. Garcia about our...our sleeping together and he said it would be all right."

Armando didn't know what to say. He wanted to sleep with Susan, he wanted to make love to her, but he didn't think he should, not until everything had been cleared up between them. "Why don't we wait a couple of days," he said, "just to make sure everything is all right."

She smiled uncertainly. "If that's what you want, Armando."

"It's not what I want, Susana, but I think it's best for now. At any rate I'd better get back to the ranch tomorrow. I've fallen behind in a lot of chores this last week."

"Yes, I suppose you have." She stared blindly at the menu and when the waiter came she ordered lamb because it was at the top of the list. It didn't matter that she didn't like lamb; whatever she ate would have seemed tasteless.

In spite of the sun, a chill ran through her body and she pulled her sweater close around her shoulders, as though to shield herself from the icy feeling that was slowly creeping around her heart.

It was late. Susan had changed into a woolly pink robe and fuzzy slippers. Armando sat next to her on the sofa, his long legs stretched out in front of him.

"If Smooch gets any closer to the fire he's going to get singed," Susan said with a smile.

"He's a funny cat but I like him." Armando curled a strand of Susan's hair around his finger. "I like you, too." He looked suddenly serious. "I love you," he said.

She touched his face. "And I love you, Armando."

"Before when I asked you to marry me you said you wanted to wait until after the baby was born." He hesitated. "If it's born the first week of April, we could be married in May."

"In May?" Relief flooded through Susan. Armando loved her; he still wanted to marry her. All of her apprehensions had been foolish. It was going to be all right after all. They'd be together; they'd be a family.

She felt aglow with love, and because she wanted to be closer she snuggled against his shoulder and looked up at him.

"I've been thinking about a honeymoon." He kissed her brow and put his arm around her. "We could go to Paris first, then on to Madrid for a week. We'd get a car there and drive on down to the south of Spain, to Marbella or Torremolinos, and rent a place on the beach for a month or two. You've had a difficult time; you need a change of scene."

Susan smiled uncertainly. "That sounds wonderful, Armando, but not very practical. With a new baby, I mean. Maybe after the baby's weaned we could go away somewhere for a few days, but—"

"Susana." Armando took a deep breath and steeled himself to say what must be said. "I love you. I love you so much that even thinking about a life without you scares me to death. I want to be married to you. I want to go to sleep with you at night and awaken with you beside me in the morning." He laced his fingers through hers. "We have to talk about the baby, Susana. About adoption."

"Adoption?" She stared at him, her amber eyes wide with surprise as joy and hope surged through her body. "You want to adopt my baby when it's born?"

His body stiffened. "No, I—" Armando clamped down hard on his lower lip and tried to suck air into his lungs. "No, I'm talking about putting the baby up for adoption."

Susan froze.

"It was brave and wonderful of you to want to have the baby, *querida*, and I admire you for that. For a while I thought I'd be able to accept the child. And I think I could have, Susana, if I hadn't met Zachary. When I did...when I saw what kind of a man he was, I knew I couldn't, that no matter how much I loved you, I could never accept a child of his."

"But it's my child. If you loved me..."

He let her go and leaned forward. He put his head in his hands, hating himself for doing this to her, but unable to stop, to change. "God, Susana," he said when he raised his face to look at her, "you know I love you. But I can't do it. It wouldn't be fair to you or to the baby. Every time I looked at the child I'd see Zachary. I don't want his child. I couldn't love it."

The color drained from Susan's face. "You—you want me to give my baby away?"

The pain he saw in her face stabbed through his body. "There are adoption agencies," he made himself say. "Here in Mexico as well as in the States. I'm sure there are good ones in Texas. You could—"

"No I couldn't! This is my baby, a part of me. I'll never give it up, not even for you."

They stared at each other. Armando said, "If you love me..."

The words hung suspended in the air.

His face was as white as hers. She saw his anguish, his pain, and for a moment she wanted to reach out to him.

"I'm sorry," he said.

Susan nodded slowly. "Yes," she said. "So am I." She pushed herself up off the sofa. "There's nothing else to talk about, is there?"

"Susana, I..." Armando shook his head. "I wish I were a better man. I wish—"

"No, don't say anything else, Armando." She turned away. "I'd like to be alone now."

"Let me stay with you tonight. I won't make love to you, Susana. But I want to hold you, to—"

She shook her head. "It's late," she said. "You have a long drive back to the ranch."

"I'll call you in the morning."

"No, don't call me."

He turned away. "Perhaps you're right," he said. "Perhaps it's better this way." He picked his leather jacket up from a chair. "Take care of yourself," he said.

"I will."

At the door he hesitated. "If you need anything—"

"I won't."

He lifted his shoulders. "Well then . . ." He hesitated. "*Vaya con Dios* Susana," he whispered. "Go with God."

Susan stood for a moment after he had left, looking at the closed door, listening for the squeak of the gate. When she heard it she winced as though she'd been struck.

At last she went over to the sofa and sat down. Smooch stretched and yawned, then left the fireplace and came to jump up on the sofa beside her. She stroked his fur as she stared into the flames.

And finally, quietly, she began to weep.

Chapter Fourteen

The cold came down hard off the mountains. January was cold, February even colder. At least twice a week the old man who sold wood brought his burro into Susan's patio, and while he sipped the steaming mug of coffee she always had ready for him, his grandson stacked the wood at the side of the house.

By the end of February it became difficult for Susan to push herself up from a chair or turn over in bed. But if at times she felt discouraged by the discomfort and by the way she looked, she had only to put her hands over her stomach and feel the movement of life there. Soon she would hold the baby in her arms, and in spite of everything that had happened, there was great joy in the thought.

Maria wrote to say that she would return to San Miguelito at the end of August and that she hoped Susan would stay until then. But Susan didn't think she would, for though she would have loved to have seen Maria, she had decided that as soon as the baby was old enough to travel she would go back to Texas. There really wasn't any reason for her to stay here now and she had decided she would go back to Granbury. She had the house there; she would get a job to support herself and the baby.

In time, maybe in fifty or sixty years if she was very very lucky, she would forget about Armando.

She had not heard from him since the night he had left her. There had been times when, hungry for the sound of his voice, she had picked up the phone. Once she had even dialed his number, but she'd hung up before it could ring.

It was over. That was something she had to face, a fact she had to live with. She loved Armando, she longed for him, but she would not sacrifice her child for him.

Inocencia and Francisco had bought a lovely colonial home in the center of San Miguelito and Susan saw Inocencia almost every day. On Sundays Inocencia and Francisco took her to Sophia's for dinner. Susan always asked Inocencia to be sure that Armando hadn't also been invited, to avoid any embarrassment for either of them.

Inocencia was furious with Armando. Even when Susan told her about Zachary and said that she could understand Armando's feelings about her unborn child, Inocencia remained unforgiving.

"If he loved you he would love your child," she said.

And to herself Susan would amend, if he loved me *enough*.

The first of March came in with northern winds from Sonora. In her eighth month now, Susan stopped going to her Spanish class. The cobblestones were difficult for her and because she was afraid she might fall, she hesitated to walk into town.

Inocencia and Francisco drove her in twice a week for groceries. And often, after she and Inocencia had shopped, they would go to the central plaza and sit on the ornate but uncomfortable iron benches and wait for Francisco.

Every evening between five-thirty and six the birds came to roost in the laurel trees. They came from every direction, split-tail grackles, wings spread, scolding in high-pitched squawks, just at the time when the bells in the big church facing the square began to ring the hour of evening Mass. This was the time of day that Susan liked best, and as the days fled past she felt a sadness deep inside her, for she had begun to love this town. It had become a part of her, as Armando had become a part of her. Soon she would leave San Miguelito, and him, but wherever she went the town, and Armando, would always be a part of her.

One late afternoon as they sat waiting for Francisco, Inocencia said, "We have set the date for the church ceremony. It will be the fifteenth of March."

"That's wonderful."

"You'll be my witness again, of course."

Susan shook her head. "I'm as big as a barn, Inocencia. I don't want to embarrass you."

"Embarrass me!" Inocencia looked shocked. "Of course you won't embarrass me. You're one of my dearest friends, Susana. If it hadn't been for you I might never have had the courage to marry Francisco. We want you with us when we marry in the church."

"But . . ." Susan looked down at her hands. "Armando will be there," she said. "It would be uncomfortable for both of us."

"But for such a short time, the ceremony and then the luncheon. Please, Susana, I want you with me. Do it for me."

And at last, although she didn't want to, Susan agreed.

The church wedding took place on a Friday morning. The temperature had dropped into the thirties during the night. It was cold outside, and almost as cold inside the church.

Susan, dressed in a royal-blue wool dress with velvet collar and cuffs, shivered while she waited in one of the side rooms of the church with Inocencia. "You certainly picked a cold day to get married," she said with a grin.

Inocencia tightened her fingers around her bouquet of lavender roses, a shade she'd selected to go with her mauve suit. "At least the guests won't know whether I'm shivering with cold or fright," she said. And when Susan looked at her, surprised, Inocencia said, "I've waited forty years for this day, Susana. The civil ceremony made our marriage legal in the eyes of the state, but it is the church ceremony I have always longed for. Now it is here and, yes, I'm so nervous I—"

The first notes of the organ sounded.

"That's our cue," Susan said just as the door opened and one of the church secretaries came in.

She smiled at both of them and said, "It is beginning, Señora Gutierez."

Susan picked up her bouquet of daisies. Then she hugged Inocencia and said, "This is it, amiga." With a nod to the secretary she went out into the church. Just then, the door on the other side of the altar opened and Armando stepped out.

For a moment Susan hesitated. It had been weeks since she'd seen him. She was large with child now, awkward and misshapen. She would not have minded him seeing her this way if they were still together, but now she was too embarrassed to look directly at him.

They came in on either side of the altar, Francisco behind him, Inocencia behind her, and stood beside the bride and groom, facing each other.

Armando had lost weight. His face was drawn and there were lines around his nose and his mouth that had not been there before. Their eyes met for a moment. Susan saw his gaze travel down her body and, self-conscious, she moved a step back so that she was a little behind Inocencia.

"Dearly beloved," Father Ramiro said. "We are gathered here together in the sight of God..."

Francisco reached for Inocencia's hand as the words, so old and yet so new, went on.

"Do you take this woman as your wife...?"

"Do you take this man as your husband...?"

Susan kept her eyes cast down. This was a joyous occasion. She must not spoil it with her tears.

"Inasmuch as these two have come together in the sight of God..."

Susan raised her head and looked at Armando. He was looking straight ahead, and there was on his face such unutterable sadness, such pain, that Susan wanted to say, No, don't look like that. It's all right. I know how you feel. I understand.

He turned. His eyes met hers for the heartbeat of a moment.

"In sickness and in health..." Father Ramiro said.

Tears for what could never be gathered in Susan's eyes. She wanted to look away but she couldn't. She was caught in the depth of Armando's Spanish-green eyes, yearning, drowning...

"In the name of the Father, the Son, and the Holy Spirit, I now pronounce you man and wife." Father Ramiro smiled. "You may kiss the bride," he said.

It was the moment of joy for the bride and groom; a moment of what might have been for Susan and Armando.

Susan turned and quickly wiped the tears away with her fingertips. The kiss ended. Armando shook Francisco's hand; Susan hugged Inocencia.

"Happiness," she said in a choked voice. "Happiness always, dear Inocencia."

There were thirty guests at the luncheon that was held at one of the restaurants on the lake. A three-tiered wedding cake graced the middle of the long table and a champagne fountain bubbled near the window.

As the best man, Armando was called upon to offer a toast. He stood and raised his glass. *"Salud, pesetas y amor,"* he said. "Health, money and love, and time to enjoy them."

Other guests offered toasts. Champagne glasses were filled and refilled. The food arrived and festive laughter rang around the table. A woman asked Susan when she was due. Before she could answer, Sophia said, "It will be soon. Two weeks at the most."

She smiled across the table at Susan. "I've knitted an afghan for the baby's bed," she said. "Pink *and* blue. I didn't want to show favoritism."

"I don't know what I'd have done without you," Susan said with a smile. "I won't have to buy any baby clothes for a year."

"Sophia is a wonderful woman," said Father Ramiro, who was sitting next to Susan. "How are you feeling, my dear?"

"Just fine, Father. Thank you."

"Have you thought about taking a room in town until after the baby is born? You're a bit isolated up on the hill. What if something should happen?"

"Nothing's going to happen," Susan assured him. "Esperanza comes every day, and I have the telephone. I can call for a taxi when it's time. Dr. Garcia says that everything is coming along according to schedule."

"Still..." Ramiro glanced across the table at Armando, and when he saw that Armando was deep in conversation with the man next to him, he said to Susan, "I'm sorry things couldn't have worked out between you and Armando."

"Some things aren't meant to be," she said carefully.

"What will you do after the baby comes?"

"Go back to Texas. I have my parents' house. I'll live there."

"It will be hard, raising a child alone."

"Perhaps." Susan took a sip of her tea. "But I'll manage." She looked across the table at Armando. He had stopped talking to the man at his side. "How are you, Susana?" he asked.

"I'm fine, Armando. Thank you."

"Do you feel all right?"

"I feel big." She summoned a smile. "Huge, voluminous, unwieldly and unattractive."

"Never unattractive," he said.

They looked at each other, and it seemed to Susan as though the buzz of conversation around them stilled and faded and they were alone.

Susan's throat constricted. "How—how is Juanita?" she asked.

"She's well. She asks about you."

"Give her my best."

"I will."

"How's Smooch?"

"He's beginning to prowl. It's hard to keep him home at night. I think he has a lady friend."

That brought the beginning of a smile. And suddenly she longed to touch him, to reach out her hand and trace the lines of his face, his full, sensuous lips. There'd been so many nights when she'd laid alone in her bed, hungering for his touch, for his warmth beside her, for the sound of his voice. Sitting across from him now and not being able to touch him was a special kind of torture.

"When is..." She saw him struggle for the words. "When is the baby due?" he asked.

"The first week of April."

"I heard Father Ramiro suggest you take a room in town. That's a good idea."

"I'd rather be in my own place."

"You're going back to Texas after it...after the baby is born?"

"Yes."

"To Houston?"

Susan shook her head. "No, to Granbury. I know people there. I'm sure I can find a job."

Armando nodded. "I suppose that's best."

He thought he would go mad if he didn't touch her, and because he knew that if he did he would be lost, he pushed his chair back from the table and said, "I'm afraid I have to leave. One of the mares is about to foal and I should be there." He hesitated. "I don't suppose you're ready to leave yet?"

"No, I . . ." Susan looked down at her plate. "Not yet," she said.

"I'll see that Susan gets safely home." Father Ramiro stood up so that he could shake hands with Armando.

And still Armando hesitated. "Well then, I'll . . . I'll just tell Inocencia and Francisco that I'm leaving." He looked down at Susan. "It's been good seeing you," he said.

"You, too." She met his gaze for a moment, then looked down at the hands clasped in her lap so that she would not see him leave.

"I'm sorry." Father Ramiro covered her hands with one of his.

"Yes," Susan said. "So am I."

Susan's body seemed to change the last week in March. She felt the baby shift and turn. It became more difficult for her to move around. It was almost impossible to sleep at night and in the morning it was all she could do to roll herself out of bed.

She saw Dr. Garcia once a week now. On the day of her appointment she tried to phone for a taxi. The line was busy every time she dialed, so finally she put on her poncho and walked in to town. She was out of breath by the time she reached the hospital and Dr. Garcia frowned when he saw her.

"Why didn't you take a taxi?" he asked. And when Susan told him she had tried but that the line had been busy, he frowned and said, "I don't like the idea of your being up there on the hill all alone."

"I'm not alone," Susan said, "except at night. And I have the phone. Believe me, doctor, one pain and I'm on the way here."

"If you can't get a taxi, call me and I'll send someone to pick you up."

"I will," she said. She liked Dr. Garcia and she had confidence in him. And while there was an uncertainty of the unknown, she wasn't afraid. She wanted this baby and she was willing to endure whatever pain was necessary to have it. She knew that Garcia was a capable doctor, and that although the hospital was small, it was well equipped.

"I'll see you next week," she said when she left.

"Or before." Garcia smiled. "It could be anytime now, Susana. The minute your pains start I want you to call me."

And again she assured him that she would.

It was raining when she left the hospital. She walked two blocks to a *sitio*, a taxi stand, but had to wait under an awning for ten minutes before a taxi came.

By the time she got up to her house, the rain had worsened. It came down in hard, blinding sheets, and she was soaked when she hurried, as fast as her bulk would allow, into the house.

The rain continued all that night and the next day. It slackened off the following day, but that night it began again. On Thursday the local radio station announced that there was concern about flooding in some of the low-lying neighborhoods of San Miguelito, and people had been evacuated to higher ground.

The rain continued all that night and the following day. On Friday afternoon when Esperanza's son came to see his mother home, he said, "The street in front of the *señorita*'s house is running with water, Mama. If we don't leave now it will be difficult to leave at all."

"I think you should go in to town and stay at a hotel, Señorita Susana." With a worried look on her face, Esperanza shook her head. "I don't like it that you will be here alone this weekend."

"I'll be perfectly all right," Susan assured her.

"But what if the baby decides to come?"

"It's not due for another week. There's plenty of food and firewood. I'll be just fine." She helped Esperanza into her *rebozo*. "You'd better go along now."

Esperanza hesitated. "Perhaps I should stay. The children can manage without me this one weekend."

"There's no need." Susan patted the other woman's shoulder. "You go along. I'll be perfectly all right. I feel absolutely wonderful."

And she did. In a burst of energy that night, she cleaned all of her dresser drawers and rearranged her closet. When that was done she refolded all of the baby clothes in the small dresser. The little outfits looked so tiny. She held up one of the sets that Sophia had knitted, a pink-and-white dress with matching booties and cap. It seemed impossible to believe that in a few more days or a week she'd actually be holding her baby in her arms.

She checked the overnight bag she'd packed to take to the hospital with her. Everything was ready, all she had to do now was wait.

When she got into bed she felt a prickly sensation in her back, but there were no pains, nothing to alarm her. She read for a little while, then turned the light off and went to sleep. When she awoke in the night her back hurt and it was more difficult than usual for her to move around.

The rain stopped in the morning but started again in the afternoon, coming down in such great slashing sheets that it was almost impossible to see across the patio. Susan built up the fire in the living room and settled down on the sofa to read.

She had her first pain a little after four that afternoon. It came out of nowhere, a great clutching stab that tore through her body and left her gasping. She sat up, hand over her belly, and waited. When it came again she pushed herself up off the sofa.

"Take it easy," she said aloud. "There's still plenty of time."

She had promised to call Inocencia before she called Dr. Garcia. It's time, she'd say. By tomorrow you'll be a godmother.

There was no answering buzz when Susan picked up the phone. She jiggled the receiver. Nothing happened. Okay, Susan, she told herself. Don't panic.

She waited ten minutes and tried the phone again. Just as she picked it up another pain hit her, whooshing the breath out of her body, making her bend double with the force of it.

The telephone was still dead.

She went to the window and looked out. The rain hadn't slackened. So she'd get wet. Big deal. She took the poncho out of the closet and put it on. Then she remembered that she had to leave food for Smooch, so she filled his dish and put water down for him, grunting as she stooped because her back felt as though someone had been beating on it with a two-by-four.

She picked up her overnight bag and got an umbrella from the closet. It was a little over a mile to town, but most of it was downhill. Her shoes were sturdy and rubber-soled. If she went slowly and cautiously she'd be all right.

The rain hit Susan hard when she closed her door and stepped into the patio. The water sloshed over her shoes but there wasn't anything to do about that, she'd have to make the best of it. She crossed the patio and when she opened the gate she stood for a moment looking out at the street, an expression of disbelief on her face. She couldn't even see the cobblestones for the torrent of water rushing down from the top of the hill.

A pain hit her again and she tightened her grip on the gate. She had to get to the hospital, had to.... She rode with the pain and when it stopped she took a deep breath and still clinging to the gate, stepped out into the street.

The whoosh of water hit and climbed as high as her knees with a terrible force. If she hadn't been hanging on to the gate she would have been washed off her feet.

Susan let go of the umbrella to get a better grip on the gate and watched horrified as the umbrella swirled around and around in a whirlpool.

Still clinging to the gate Susan managed to get herself back into the patio. She knew now that she'd never be able to walk into town.

Don't panic, she told herself again as she made her way back toward the house. You'll be all right if you don't panic. Other women have had babies unattended, you can, too. Maybe the phone will be connected in a little while. Maybe you're not really in labor—

A pain knifed through her and she said, "Or maybe you are."

By the time Susan got into the house she was soaked through to the skin. She went into the bedroom and standing in front of the fire, she stripped out of her clothes and towel-dried her hair. She put on a clean nightgown and robe and set about doing the things she thought should be done.

She pulled back the bottom sheet and covered the bed with newspapers before she tugged the sheet back into place. Then she got a stack of towels from the linen closet and a receiving blanket from the baby's dresser. What else? She thought for a moment, then went to get a pair of scissors, some string and a bottle of alcohol.

With a lot of huffing and puffing, she managed to push an end table from the living room into the bedroom. She shoved it close to the bed and put all of the things she'd gotten together on it.

She wished she knew more about childbirth.

Ten minutes later she tried the phone again. It was still dead.

The lights began to flicker when she turned them on, so she got out the candles and matches in case she needed them. At seven o'clock she made herself a cup of tea, and when she finished it, she began to pace up and down in front of the living room fire. She knew now that she should have taken a room in town as everyone had suggested. She should have let Esperanza stay. She should have...

But all the should haves in the world weren't going to do her any good now. She was on her own.

By nine o'clock Susan felt as though her back had been broken. The pains came intermittently. She thought she should lie down but she was afraid if she did she wouldn't be able to get up again, so she paced, up and down the living room, into the kitchen, into the bedroom, yipping in pain every time a contraction came.

The lights flickered again. She put three candles into the candelabra, placed a box of matches beside it and prayed the lights wouldn't go out.

The pains were harder now and when they came they lasted longer. She'd read that women who had natural childbirth were supposed to pant, and that's what she tried to do. Puff, puff, puff. It didn't take the pain away.

If only the rain would stop. If only... She held her breath, listening because she thought she'd heard someone running across the patio. She went to the door but before she could call out, Armando shouted, "Susana! Susana!"

With a glad cry she opened the door.

He stood there, drenched, water running down over his head.

"Armando!" She'd never been so glad to see anybody in her life. She grabbed his arm. "Come in," she said. "I'm so glad you're here...." She tried to pull him into the house.

"No, my shoes—"

"I don't care about your shoes." She pulled him inside and closed the door, so happy to see him she wanted to throw herself into his arms.

He took off his shoes, then his raincoat. "I've never seen it rain like this," he said. "The streets are flooded in town and the road's washed out two miles back." He looked at Susan. "Are you all right? I thought about you being alone here over the weekend and I—"

She gasped and clutched his arm for support. "Look," she managed to say when the pain receded, "I've been having pains since this afternoon. The phone's out. I thought I could walk into town but the water's too deep. You'd better get me to the hospital right away."

Armando stared at her. "You're sure?"

"You bet I'm sure!"

Armando ran a hand through his damp hair. *"Por Dios,"* he said.

Susan looked at him, not understanding.

"The pickup stalled out a couple of miles back. I walked here. We couldn't make it back to town, Susana, not in your condition."

"But I . . ." She took a deep breath. "What do you know about delivering babies?"

He stared at her. A cold wave of fear washed over him. "Not a hell of a lot," he said. Then, seeing how frightened Susan was, he forced a smile. "But I've helped my mares. Maybe it's not too different."

"Maybe not." Valiantly Susan met his smile. The pain hit her again and she doubled over.

"We'd better get you into bed." Armando put his arm around her.

He still wasn't sure what had made him come tonight. He hadn't called Susan in all the time they'd been apart, but because of the rain he'd tried to call her tonight. The phone had been dead when he'd picked it up and that had scared him. He'd thought, What if she's alone this weekend? What if the baby comes?

He'd gone to Sophia's first because he knew that Susana sometimes spent the weekend with the elderly lady. But Susana hadn't been there, so he'd driven to San Miguelito. He went to Inocencia and Francisco's new house, but Susana hadn't been there, either.

"Maybe I'd better go with you," Inocencia said when Armando told her he was going to Susan's.

"There's no need for you to go out in this weather," he'd said. "I just want to make sure she's all right."

"After almost two months?" Inocencia had glared at him.

He hadn't answered her and when he turned away, Inocencia said, "Stop on your way back and let me know how she is, Armando."

He'd nodded, then he'd hurried through the rain to the pickup. Five minutes later he'd run into a wall of water and the pickup had died.

He didn't blame Inocencia for being angry, Armando thought as he helped Susana into the bedroom. Even though he'd known it was over between them, he should have helped her. He should have been there for her. If anything happened to Susan now— He clenched his jaw. But nothing was going to happen to her.

He'd told her that he helped his mares to foal, and that was true, but usually he'd only been assisting the veterinarian. Once or twice the vet hadn't arrived on time and he'd taken over.

But it wasn't a mare this time, it was Susan.

There wasn't anyone else to help her. It was up to him.

Chapter Fifteen

At first the contractions weren't so bad. Each time one came, Susan grasped Armando's hand and hung on as tightly as she could. She tried to remember to pant, but sometimes the pains were so bad she couldn't remember anything.

Armando twisted two sheets and tied them at either end of the bed. "Later, when you have to, you can pull on these," he said.

"Okay." Susan took a deep breath. "It's going to be all right, Armando. Women have been doing this forever, you know."

"I know." He made himself smile.

But Susana wasn't any woman, she was Susana and she was in pain and he'd never been so afraid in his life. He wasn't sure he'd know what to do when the time came. What if it wasn't an easy birth? What if there were complications? *Por Dios*, what if something happened to her? It would be his fault. If he had loved her enough, if he had—

"I'm so glad you're here," she said.

"I should have come sooner."

"No, it's all right. I understand why you didn't. I—" She grimaced in pain and reached for Armando's hand. When the pain ebbed she said, "That was a real doozy."

He didn't know the word, but he nodded and said, "You're being awfully brave."

"I don't feel brave." Susan took a deep breath. "Shouldn't you be boiling water or something?"

"I don't think so, not yet."

"Here comes another one." Susan started panting as the pain tore into her. When it stopped she tried to stretch and pressed her hand against the small of her back.

"Would you like me to rub your back?" Armando asked.

"Yes, please. It feels like it's going to break in two."

He turned her a little to her side and began to gently massage her. "How's that? Does it help?"

"Oh yes," she murmured. "That feels so good."

He rubbed her back between pains, and when she insisted on getting up to walk, he walked with her. When the pains became more severe she lay down again.

It was long after midnight when Armando gave her the roped sheets to pull on. He had taken off his jacket and rolled his sleeves up, but other than to build up the fire in both the living room and the bedroom, there was little he could do except sit beside her and hold her hand when the pains came or rub her back to ease the strain there.

One o'clock came, and two. She could hear the rain still beating hard against the windows. Once in a while thunder crashed and lightning flashed across the room, and when it did the lights flickered.

Susan was very tired. Armando bathed her face, and when she released the sheets he massaged her hands. She'd been in labor for more than eight hours. He'd heard of women who were in labor for two or three days with a first baby. She couldn't go on that long; she wouldn't be able to stand it.

He debated going down to the hospital for help. He thought he could make it, but he didn't know how long it would take. He suggested it and Susan said, "No, please don't leave me, Armando. What if the baby should come? I can't do this alone. Please stay here with me."

She wasn't sure why Armando had come; she only knew how thankful she was that he had. He would leave her again when this was over—if it ever was over—but all that mattered was that he was with her now.

The rain slashed hard against the windows and she wondered if it would ever stop. In the distance she heard another roll of thunder, then the lights flickered and went out.

Armando cursed. But he said, "It's all right," and Susan heard him strike a match. Then he lighted the candelabra on the stand beside the bed.

This was bad; it made it harder. He wouldn't be able to see when the baby came.

"I'm going to get more candles," he told Susan.

"There's another candelabra on the dining room table." She shifted in bed and tried to look at the clock. When she saw that it was after three she said, as though to reassure him, "It will be light soon, Armando."

The pains grew harder, fiercer. Susan pulled on the bed sheets, half pulling herself up and moaning with pain each time a contraction came. Sometimes, unable to hold back, she cried aloud. "Sorry," she'd say then. "Sorry about that."

Armando wiped the sweat from her face. "Howl if you want to," he told her, and tried to smile reassuringly. But his insides twisted with anguish. God, how he hated to see her suffer. She shouldn't have to go through this; no one should have to endure such pain.

There were moments when Susan was in the throes of a contraction that Armando's thoughts turned murderous. Zachary Owens had done this to her, he was the cause of all of Susana's suffering. I'll go to Houston when this is over, he told himself. I'll find him and I'll kill him.

"So tired," she whispered.

"I know, *querida*."

"Glad you're here."

"So am I." He brushed the damp hair back from her forehead.

"It won't be much longer, will it, Armando?"

"I don't think so."

"Maybe you'd better boil that water now."

"I will in a little while."

"It's almost daylight. I hope it's daylight when the baby comes."

He raised the candelabra above the bed. "Let me have a look," he said.

There was a part of Susan that recoiled at the idea of Armando's seeing her like this. But there was nothing else to do. He'd said he had helped foals into the world, now he would help her baby.

"Listen," she said when he came back beside her again, "if anything happens to me—"

"Nothing is going to happen to you."

"Just in case..." Susan grasped his hand. "Just in case, Armando." A pain came. She rode it out. "I should have spoken to Inocencia, but I didn't.... If anything happens to me—" Her hand tightened in his. "Ask her, ask Inocencia to take the baby."

Armando felt as though someone had taken hold of his heart and twisted it. He bit hard on the inside of his cheek and said, "Nothing is going to happen to you, Susana. You're going to have a fine, healthy baby, and both of you—"

"Promise me," she said.

Armando took a deep breath. "I promise," he said.

She lay back. "Don't look so upset. That's a just-in-case thing." She turned toward the window. "Is it morning yet?"

"Almost."

"I don't hear the rain."

"I think it finally stopped."

"Do you think this will be over soon? I—" Another pain slashed through her body. She screamed, "Do something! Please, oh, please make it stop. Oh, God, I hurt!"

Armando grasped her hand. "I know," he said.

But he couldn't know. All he could do was watch her face contort with pain and tell her how brave she was.

She made no attempt to hold back her panting cries now. She focused on her pain, rode with it, hated it.

Armando raised the sheet off her knees. "I can see the head," he said. "You have to push, Susana."

"I can't."

"Yes, you can! Push, Susana. Push hard now."

She took a deep breath. She closed her eyes and pushed with every bit of her strength.

"That's it," Armando said. "Once more, Susana. Once more, *querida*."

She felt an all-encompassing pain, hot, angry, a pain that slashed her body in two.

"Yes!" Armando cried. "Yes, love, it's here, love!"

He held her child in his hands, warm and wet and unbelievably tiny. He had heard that you were supposed to slap a baby to make it cry, but the thought of striking anything so small terrified him. He turned the baby over. It was a girl. She didn't cry, she didn't make a sound.

"Oh, God," he whispered. He reached into the tiny mouth and cleaned the mucus there. She didn't breathe. He laid her on the bed and tilting her head, he covered her mouth and nose with his and very gently puffed his breath into her body.

"What is it?" Susan tried to sit up. "Is something wrong?"

He breathed into the tiny body again. The chest raised. She breathed. She began to howl.

Armando held her against him. "It's a girl," he said. There was wonder in his voice. "You have a baby girl, Susana." He laid the baby on her stomach.

Susan looked at the baby. "I have a girl?"

"Yes, dear."

She touched the small head. The little red face squinched and the baby howled. Susan's eyes widened. What she felt mostly at this moment was surprise. The baby was here! She had a baby!

Happy tears ran down her face. Almost afraid to touch this delicate new person, she ran her fingers over the curly blond fuzz on the small head. That made her smile. "Is she all right?" she asked Armando.

"She's perfect," he said.

There was something in his voice that stilled the hand caressing the baby's back. She looked at him and there was an expression in his eyes that she had never seen before. I wish she were yours, she wanted to say. Oh, how I wish she were yours.

She lifted the baby onto her chest. Armando cut and tied the cord. He pushed on Susan's stomach. She felt a tug and a sense of relief.

"I'm going to bathe her now," Armando said. He picked the baby up. "Rest, Susana. I'll be back in a little while."

He wrapped the baby girl in one of the towels Susan had put on the table near the bed, and picking up a receiving blanket, he carried the child into the kitchen. He laid her on the counter while he ran warm water into the dish pan, then very carefully he began to bathe her. She howled, eyes closed, kicking her feet. He looked at her toes. How could anything be so small? So perfect?

When Armando dried her off he wrapped her in the receiving blanket and picked her up in his arms. She stopped crying and opened her eyes. She looked up at him. Something squeezed at his heart. He held her so her cheek was against his. He felt her warmth, her aliveness. Susana's baby, he thought. This is Susana's baby.

When he took her into the bedroom she began to cry again. Susan opened her eyes. "I fell asleep," she said with a smile. "I just floated off. It was wonderful." She held out her arms for the baby. She started to cry and Susan said, "Oh, don't cry." She kissed the soft cheek. "What should I do? Is something wrong? What's the matter?"

"I think she's hungry," Armando said.

"Oh." Susan looked up at him. "Then I should...I should feed her, shouldn't I?"

He helped her to sit up and pushed the pillows behind her back for support. "I think you'd better," he said.

Susan cuddled the baby against her. She was scared. She wondered if she'd ever be able to do all of the things new mothers did, if she'd ever know how to take proper care of this precious bundle she held in her arms.

"Let me help you." Armando knelt beside the bed. Very gently he took her breast and brushed the nipple against the baby's cheek and toward her mouth. He rubbed the nipple against the baby's lips, and suddenly she stopped crying and began to nurse.

"Oh, my goodness." The strangest feeling welled up inside Susan. She looked at Armando with an expression of wonder on her face. "She's taking it."

The breath caught in his throat as he gazed down at mother and daughter. He knew that never in his life had he seen anything as beautiful as Susan and her newborn child. The baby's hand rested against its mother's breast, the rosebud mouth was pink against the creamy fullness.

And because Armando wanted this child to be his, tears clogged his throat and he turned away and left the room before Susan could see them.

She stared at his retreating back. He had turned away from her. He didn't want to see her nurse the baby. She kissed the top of the baby's head. "It's all right," she whispered. "I love you. We're going to be all right."

Armando leaned his head against the fireplace. Hot tears coursed down his face and he knotted his fists against his eyes to try to stop them. He cursed himself for every day he had been away from Susana, for not being there to help her when she tried to push herself up out of a chair or stoop to pick something up. His stomach tightened with fear at the thought of what might have happened if he hadn't come yesterday.

He'd been cold and heartless, blaming her for not wanting to give her child up, hating the unborn child because it had been fathered by Zachary Owens and not by him. He ground his fist into the hard stone and cursed himself. How could he have done that to Susana? He loved her. Oh, dear God, he loved her so.

At last Armando pushed himself away from the fireplace. He went into the kitchen and began to fix tea and toast for Susan. He had just put the things on a tray when someone knocked, and he heard Inocencia call out, "Susana? Susana, are you there?"

He hurried into the living room and opened the door. "Thank God you're here," he said when he saw his aunt and Francisco.

"You were supposed to come right back and let me know how Susana was," she said accusingly. "Why didn't you come? Why...?" She looked up at him. She saw the patches of fatigue under eyes red from crying. With a hand to her breast she gasped. "What is it?" she asked. "What has happened?"

"It's all right. Susana has had the baby. Everything's all right now."

"Did you...? *Dios mio*, Armando, did you deliver it?"

He nodded. "Why don't you go in?" he said. "She'll want to see you."

"Is it a boy or girl?"

"A girl." A smile tugged at Armando's mouth. "A very tiny little girl." He handed her the tea tray.

Inocencia smiled. "That's what I hoped for all along," she said.

When she went into the bedroom, Francisco said, "You look like you could use a cup of coffee."

"Yes, I guess I could." Armando ran a hand across his face. "It's been a long night."

"Is Susana really all right?"

Armando nodded. "I'll walk into town to the hospital. It's stopped raining so maybe the roads are passable now. I'll have Garcia drive up and take a look at her."

The two men went into the kitchen, and when Armando had had a cup of coffee he said, "I'd better get going. I want to check on the pickup, too. Tell Susana..." He hesitated. "Tell Susana I'll see her later."

"I will. She's a wonderful young woman. I hope things work out for her."

Armando nodded. "Yes, so do I," he said.

The church smelled of dampness and dripping wax. He walked down a side aisle, the sound of his footsteps too loud in the silent church.

He entered a pew, to the side and in the middle, and went down on his knees to pray. But the words of the prayer were difficult to form. "Please," he whispered. "Forgive," he said. He rested his head against the back of his hands and tried to focus his thoughts. Let Susana and the child be all right. The child. A soft moan escaped his lips. Never in his life had he experienced the fear he'd known when he realized the baby wasn't breathing. Nor had he ever felt such joy as when it began to cry.

Armando stayed there on his knees for a long time, and at last peace, like a warm hand upon his shoulder, flowed through him. He got up then and when he left the pew, he took some coins from his pocket and went to light two candles, one for Susana and one for her child.

Just as he turned to leave, he heard a door open at the back of the church and then he saw Father Ramiro walking toward him. "Is that you, Armando?" Ramiro asked, squinting through the dimness. "Is anything wrong?"

"Susana had her baby last night," Armando said. "It was a little girl. I delivered her."

"You...?" Father Ramiro stared at him. "*You* delivered the baby?"

Armando nodded. "It was..." He swallowed hard. "It was quite an experience."

"I should imagine! How is Susana?"

"She's fine. At least I think she is. I stopped at the hospital on the way here. Dr. Garcia's with her now. And Inocencia and Francisco are there."

"Are you all right?" Ramiro rested a hand on Armando's shoulder. "You look done in."

"Yes, I'm tired." Armando flexed his shoulders. "It was a long night."

"What are you going to do now? Would you like some breakfast?"

Armando shook his head. "I'm going back to the ranch. I have some things to do."

He knew that Father Ramiro was curious, that he wanted to know how Armando had come to be with Susan, how he felt about the baby now that she was here. But he didn't want to talk about it, not yet. He needed to be alone for a little while.

"If there's anything I can do..."

"I know." Armando smiled at his friend.

"Are you sure everything's all right?"

Armando nodded. "I'll see you later and we'll talk," he said.

Susan knew that Armando wouldn't return. He had helped her when she needed him. He had been loving and kind; he had done more for her than anyone had ever done. If it hadn't been for him, both she and the baby might have died. She could ask no more. And yet . . .

What had she expected? That he would look at her child and fall instantly in love? Things didn't always work out the way you wanted them to.

Dr. Garcia came. "Everything's fine," he said when he checked both Susan and the baby. "She's a beautiful girl, looks just like you."

"She does, doesn't she?"

"Have you picked out a name for her yet?"

Susan looked at Inocencia. "I've been thinking of Hortensia," she said with a laugh.

Garcia wanted to send a nurse to stay with Susan for a few days, but Inocencia wouldn't hear of it. "I've taken care of all my nieces and nephews," she said. "I can certainly take care of Susana and the baby."

That afternoon while Susan rested, Inocencia made chicken soup. When Susan woke up she took a tray in to her. The baby lay sleeping in a crib beside the bed and Inocencia rubbed a finger over her cheek. "She's so small," she whispered. "And so perfect." She looked at Susan. "Thank God Armando was here."

"Yes," Susan said. "Thank God." She looked at her friend. "He was wonderful, Inocencia. I don't know how he managed, how he knew to do all the right things. When the pains were bad he held my hand. He did everything for me." She closed her eyes. "Everything."

"Because he loves you," Inocencia said softly. "Perhaps now that the baby is here, it will work out between the two of you, Susana."

But Susan shook her head. "No," she said. "Armando did what had to be done. Then he left, without telling me goodbye. Nothing has changed, Inocencia. He won't be back."

Armando came in the early evening. Inocencia let him in. "I wondered where you had gone," she said.

"I went back to the ranch. I took a nap, but I'm afraid I slept longer than I intended to." He put his leather jacket over a chair but held on to the package he was carrying. "How is she?" he asked.

"She's fine. She's been sleeping, but she's awake now. Why don't you go in?"

Armando nodded. "Thank you for staying with her, Tia," he said.

Inocencia shrugged. "I love Susana."

"So do I." He turned and went into the bedroom.

The baby was nursing, her rosy mouth pressed against Susan's breast, her tiny fingers against Susan's throat. Susan wore a crisp white gown tucked with lace around the neck and sleeves. The baby wore a long white shirt and a small flannel cap.

Armando stood for a moment looking at mother and child. He must have sighed, must have made a sound of some kind, because Susan raised her head and looked at him.

"Hello, Armando," she said softly, and covered her bare breast with the sheet.

He crossed the room in two strides. "No," he said, "don't cover yourself. I want to see you. I want to see our daughter."

"Armando..." His name trembled on her lips.

He sat beside Susan. "Let me see her."

Susan drew back the blanket. "Forgive me," he said to the child.

Tears filled Susan's eyes. She had dreamed of this moment, prayed for this moment, but she had not really believed it would ever come. She reached for his hand. "Oh, Armando," she said. "Armando."

"I've been so wrong. I didn't know...." He touched the top of the baby's head. "When I first held her I knew that she was a part of you and nothing that had gone before mattered. There wasn't any yesterday, there was only today, and all of our tomorrows."

He wiped her tears away with his fingertips. "I'm sorry that I hurt you," he said.

"That doesn't matter now."

The baby had fallen asleep on her breast, and when Susan straightened she said, "Can you hold her for a minute?"

Armando took the child, and as he looked down at her he knew that she was his, for she belonged to Susan, she was a part of Susan, and Susan was a part of him.

"Have you decided on a name?" he asked.

Susan shook her head. "I've been thinking about names all day, but I haven't been able to come up with anything I really like."

"My grandmother's name was Sarah. I know it's an old-fashioned name, but—"

"Sarah." She tested the name, then she curled her fingers around his and said, "Yes, that's perfect. I love it."

Holding the baby in the crook of his arm he handed the package to Susan.

"A present?" She smiled and quickly pushed the tissue aside. When she lifted the white lace christening gown from the box she looked at Armando, wonder and love and tears shining in her eyes.

"It's the dress I was christened in," he said softly. "I'd like Sarah to be christened in it." He put one arm around Susan; the other arm held the child. And he knew, in that one perfect moment, that he held the world, his world, in his arms.

"I love you," Susan said. And his world was complete.

Epilogue

The wedding party gathered around the baptismal font. Sun shone through the stained-glass windows above them and cast a glow of amber and golden light.

Baby Sarah wore her father's christening dress and a pink bow in the curly ruff of her blond hair.

The godparents, Inocencia and Francisco, stood beside Susan and Armando. Francisco held the baby.

"Sarah Elizabeth Cobian," Father Ramiro said, "I baptize you in the name of the Father, the Son, and the Holy Spirit." He sprinkled the holy water. At the small splash of water Sarah pursed her lips and made a face.

But as the other words were spoken she let out a howl as though to say, enough is enough. Let's get this over with.

Armando took her from Francisco's arms. "Shh, sweet love," he whispered. "Shh, little Sarita."

She made a small sound, half smothered cry, half contented gurgle. Then she reached for her father's finger and tightened her own fingers around it.

And as it happened every time she looked at him, every time he picked her up, Armando felt something warm and wonderful clutch at his heart. For this was his daughter. He had brought her into the world, he had given her his breath and she was his. Nothing that had gone before mattered.

He cradled her close as he put his arm around Susan, his wife, his love. My family, he thought, and bowed his head as the final blessing was given.

* * * * *

Silhouette Special Edition

COMING NEXT MONTH

#619 THE GIRL MOST LIKELY TO—Tracy Sinclair
Kate Beaumont was desperate for a man—even if she had to hire one!—for her high school reunion. And after seeing the shy, sexy scientist in distress, Garrett Richmond gladly offered his masculine services...

#620 NO PLACE TO HIDE—Celeste Hamilton
Urban refugee Carly Savoy thought she had found safety in her secluded mountain retreat—until mysterious Ben Jamison shattered her sanctuary and threatened to unravel her innermost secrets.

#621 ALL WE KNOW OF HEAVEN—Phyllis Halldorson
After seven agonizing years of grief and regret, Michaela Tanner forced herself to assume the worst about her P.O.W. husband, Heath. But on the eve of her second marriage, Heath's presence was more than mere memory...

#622 PETTICOAT LAWYER—Kate Meriwether
Camille Clark rallied all the toughness she could muster to face police officer Pike Barrett in court. But Pike, detecting softness beneath the stunning attorney's brittle sophistication, was determined not to remain her adversary for long!

#623 FREEDOM'S JUST ANOTHER WORD—Jennifer Mikels
The only thing conservative Joshua Fitzhugh shared with free-spirited Allison Gentry was his boardinghouse bathroom. But in his search for a "suitable" mate, the sensible professor was hopelessly sidetracked by his offbeat neighbor!

#624 OLD ENOUGH TO KNOW BETTER—Pamela Toth
One decade after escaping a domestic dead end, Maureen Fletcher remained blissfully single. Then her heart was hooked by handsome Bailey McGuire—but, at her age, could she handle ready-made motherhood?

AVAILABLE THIS MONTH:

COMING SOON...

For years Harlequin and Silhouette novels have been taking readers places—but only in their imaginations.

This fall look for PASSPORT TO ROMANCE, a promotion that could take you around the corner or around the world!

Watch for it in September!

★